Daniel L. Gifford

Every-Day Life in Korea

A Collection of Studies and Stories

Daniel L. Gifford

Every-Day Life in Korea
A Collection of Studies and Stories

ISBN/EAN: 9783743394827

Manufactured in Europe, USA, Canada, Australia, Japa

Cover: Foto ©Andreas Hilbeck / pixelio.de

Manufactured and distributed by brebook publishing software (www.brebook.com)

Daniel L. Gifford

Every-Day Life in Korea

A Mountain Pavilion.

Every-Day Life in Korea

A Collection of
Studies and Stories

By Rev. Daniel L. Gifford

Eight Years a Missionary in Korea

Fleming H. Revell Company

Chicago : New York : Toronto

Publishers of Evangelical Literature

PREFACE

The author has had in mind a number of classes of readers in the preparation of this book; among others, business men, fond of facts in a compact form, ladies in the missionary societies, ever alert to add to their fund of missionary information, and another class still, found in the young people's societies, who enjoy information presented in a pictorial or narrative form. We all are fond of hearing of things that have a human interest; and we like to know how other people live their lives and do their work in the world, especially if their experiences and environments are quite different from our own. The pages that follow may be characterized, in the main, as a series of pictures of life in Korea—life in the olden time, as history has presented it; modern, every-day life, as the Westerner living among an Oriental people sees it; life as it is affected by the work of the Christian missionary; and, finally, the life of the missionary himself. The author acknowledges his indebtedness for much of suggestion and material to the writings of others who have dealt with things Korean—"Corea, the Hermit Nation," by Rev. W. E. Griffis, D.D.; "Korea from its Capital," by Rev. George W. Gilmore; "Korea and her Neighbors," by Mrs. Isabella Bird Bishop;

the "Encyclopedia of Missions;" the "Seoul Independent;" the "Korean Repository."

In one respect, however, this book will be observed to differ from all the other volumes upon
Korea that have preceded it, and that is in the
proportion of its pages devoted to a presentation
of the missionary work of the land. Here it will
be found that the work has been traced historic-
ally from its beginnings, its many-sided development fully portrayed, with a chapter at the close
on that glorious, evangelistic, forward movement
now in progress in the country, the spread of
which continually reminds the workers on the
field that in a very peculiar manner they are
"laborers together with God."

DANIEL L. GIFFORD.

MENDOTA, ILL., NOV., 1897.

CONTENTS.

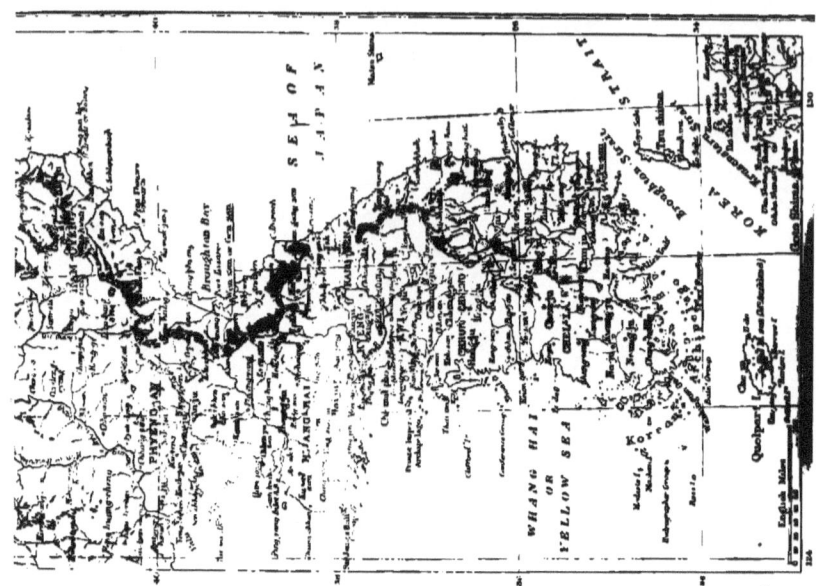

Every-day Life in Korea

CHAPTER I

WHERE IS KOREA?

A friend and myself, returning to America after our first term of missionary service in Korea, sat one Saturday evening in the office of a hotel in Salt Lake City. In signing the hotel register an hour previous, we had each of us written in the column intended for addresses, simply the word designating the country from which we had so recently arrived. A thoughtful look came over my companion's face, and presently he remarked as we sat there: "I think we made a mistake in signing that hotel register. The clerk will not know where Korea is; will think that we have given a false address and will become suspicious of us, under the impression that we are trying to swindle the hotel." A moment later I glanced toward the desk and, sure enough, the forefinger of the clerk was gently waving to and fro unmistakably in our direction. A moment later I stood at the desk. "Korea, Korea" (in a

tone of soliloquy), "where is Korea?"   I
answered, "You surely must know where Korea
is—the scene of the late war in the Far East."
"Oh," was his reply, "I never before saw it
spelled with a K." He smiled, and evidently his
mind was relieved. Allow me to remark, parenthetically, that the up-to-date spelling of the
name of the country, followed by all who reside
there, is K-o-r-e-a, with a "K."   With all the
gratuitous advertising given the country by the
comparatively recent Chino-Japanese war, it is a
matter of surprise that so many people at home
persist in thinking of Korea as an "island" located
somewhere "in the tropics."   In view of this
fact a brief study of the geography of the country
may not be out of place in this opening chapter.

Directly west from the crescent-shaped Hondo,
the largest of the islands of Japan, lies the long
and narrow peninsula of Korea. With no very
great strain upon the imagination one may see, in
the contour of the country, the resemblance to a
rabbit sitting erect.   If, too, we may take for our
conception of the modest little animal, Joel
Chandler Harris' portrait of "Br'er Rabbit," in
his fascinating animal tales, the analogy may
likewise hold true of the character of the people,
who, in the main, are mild-mannered, interesting,
keen of intellect and bright, especially in the
arts of deception. "Br'er Rabbit he lay low."

Draw a line from Milwaukee to Atlanta, and
you have about the range of the latitude of the

country; viz., from about 34 to 43 degrees north
latitude. But as the far north of the country is
prodigiously mountainous and but little popu-
lated, it is well to associate the relative position of
Korea on the map with the Ohio valley, plus
Tennessee. Seoul (pronounced by many Sah-
oul), the capital, in every way the most important
city of the peninsula, containing perhaps 200,000
people, is in the same latitude, as Mr. Gilmore
suggests, as the city of Richmond, Virginia. So
it will be seen that Korea and the tropics are a
long way apart, if tigers *do* exist there. In the
absence of statistical bureaus, such as are found
in western lands, it is impossible to lay claim to
scientific accuracy in speaking of the size of the
country; but Korea with its islands has probably
an area of ninety thousand square miles, equivalent to that of the states of New York and
Pennsylvania combined.

Probably twelve million people are scattered
through the valleys of the Hermit Kingdom.

The visitor to Korea journeys, as does almost
everyone, by a Japanese steamer of the Nippon
Yusen Kaishia line, from Nagasaki, Japan, which
first touches at the southeastern port of Korea—
Fusan. Thence to Chemulpo, the seaport of
Seoul, half-way up the western coast, the steamer
threads its way through a profusion of islands,
washed by dangerous currents. Off the south
and west coasts of Korea lie thousands of islands,
whose waters teem with fish. Indeed, one of the

titles of the King of Korea is "Lord of the Ten Thousand Islands." These islands are mostly mountainous, many of them sheer rocks, while others are covered with vegetation. The largest of these is Quelpart, the "Botany Bay" of Korea, and probably the best known is "Port Hamilton," at one time an English possession. Along the eastern coast, it is worthy of remark, islands are exceedingly rare. Hon. C. Waeber, the former Russian minister, in his admirable paper on the meteorology of Korea, speaks of the cold Arctic current flowing down the eastern coast of the country; but the southern and western coasts are washed by the same Yellow Sea which laves the shore of northern China, and the waters off these two coasts feel the influence of one of the three branches of the warm Japanese Current, which corresponds to the Gulf Stream flowing in the Atlantic Ocean.

The coast is rather bleak and forbidding, giving but little idea of the fine scenery existing in the interior. Frequent inlets break the coast line, especially on the west and south sides of the country, in the smaller of which at one time of the day may be seen a broad sheet of dancing water, with boats laden with brush and rice, flitting hither and thither; but seen at a later hour, a transformation has taken place and the eye rests on dreary mud-flats, with a junk here and there standing high and dry on the plain, or resting in the channel of a very modest creek.

Crab-holes are much in evidence. Wading-birds utter their sharp cries, and yonder the smoke curls from the rude hut of the salt-refiner. This transformation scene has been wrought by the tide, which rises along these coasts, somewhat as it does in the Bay of Fundy, to an average height of twenty-six feet. On the eastern coast, be it noted in contrast, there is a rise and fall in the tide of a very few feet only. The interior of the country is a perfect checker-board of mountains; for, in traveling from one end of the land to the other, a person is never out of their sight. The mountains are chiefly composed of gneiss, various schists and granite, which in the lower peaks and hilltops are mostly in a disintegrated form. The soil of mountain and valley is generally yellow in color, but certain of the peaks are black, as are some of the river plains. These picturesque mountains, of every shape and size, are frequently verdureless, with many a furrow cut into their surface by the heavy rainfall of the summer. Others are covered wholly or in part with pine shrubs or trees, as well as grass and bushes of the magenta-hued azalea. The only snow-capped peaks, to my knowledge, are found in the Ever-White Mountains, upon the northern frontier. A high ridge of mountains traverses the peninsula somewhat close to the eastern coast, forming a watershed with a short slope to the east and a long slope to the west, between it and the partially enveloping sea. From this range lateral

spurs run out.   The influence of this range upon
the country is seen in the fact that, with the
exception of the two southeastern provinces (produced by the range veering over more toward the
middle of the country, as it nears the south, in
latitude 37 degrees), most of the larger rivers and
the bulk of the population are to be found on the
western side of the peninsula.   This illustration
I have heard used: The distribution of the population of Korea may be compared to an open fan,
with the handle to the east and the slats project-
ing toward the Yellow Sea, the first in order
being the southeast provinces of North and South
Kyeng Sang.

The most important stream is the Yalu River,
off whose mouth occurred the one important naval
engagement in the recent war.   This river,
together with the Tumen River and the Ever-
White Mountains, forms the northern boundary
of Korea, between China on the north and the
territory of Russia on the northeast.   Other
important rivers there are, which, however, do
not compare in length with the one first mentioned—the Tatong River, in the north, upon
which the city of Pyeng-yang (pronounced Ping-
yang) is located; further south the Han River,
which bends around the city of Seoul; and still
further south the Keum River, all of which are
on the west side of the peninsula.   In the southeast of Korea, also worthy of mention, is the Naktong River.   The treaty ports of Korea consist of

Seoul, Chemulpo, and Fusan, already mentioned, and Gensan on the eastern coast. Two new ports have been opened this autumn—one at Mokpo in the southwest, the other at Chinampo, the seaport of Pyeng-yang.

Korea, for many centuries, consisted of eight provinces, but about a year ago, for administrative purposes, five of the largest were cut in two, making a total of thirteen provinces. The historical eight, with their subdivisions, are located as follows: In the northeast are the provinces of North and South Ham Kyeng; in the northwest are North and South Pyeng An; below them, in the western central portion, lies Whang Hai, then Kyeng Kui, then North and South Choung Chong; in the eastern middle part is Kang Won; in the southeast lie North and South Kyeng Sang; and in the southwest are North and South Chulla.

The remark upon the country which seems to call forth the greatest surprise at home is, that in the winter time I frequently have seen oxen, each laden with a couple of great bags of rice, walking across the Han River, near Seoul, upon the ice.

Further than this, now and again, when taking a Saturday afternoon half-holiday skating upon the same river, I have seen a hundred men and boys at a time grouped on the ice, half of them standing about with their long-stemmed pipes, the other half seated upon little hand-

sleds, each beside a small square hole in the ice
and in his hands a square-framed reel, with which
he worked up and down a heavily weighted three-
pronged trolling-hook, in the water below.
Their success in fishing, it may be mentioned,
seemed to be rather similar to that of the majority of men who invest in lottery tickets. But the
point to be noted is that the ice was frozen to
such a thickness that, with a hundred or more
men massed in one spot, it neither broke nor
cracked. Winter settles down by the middle of
December. In the central and southern parts of
the country the thermometer ranges down to
zero; farther north, in the vicinity of Pyeng-yang,
the mercury has been known to fall as low as fifteen
degrees below zero, Fahrenheit. What the cold
lacks in thermometer readings it seems to make
up in a certain penetrating quality. In the
neighborhood of Seoul there is an occasional snow-
fall of perhaps six inches. By the middle of
February the weather begins to moderate, and
by the middle of the following month the farmers
are mending the banks of the rice fields and
beginning their spring work. The spring and fall
in Korea are long and delightful, with any number of beautiful clear days. But what shall I say
of the rainy season of midsummer?

Think of the fall of rain in the heaviest summer
storm at home, and that is the way it will pour
for half a day at a time. There will be clouds
with recurring showers for one or two weeks.

TOILERS OF THE FIELDS.

Tiled roofs begin to leak. Here a mud wall, there the thatched roof of some poor Korean, falls with a crash. Streets and drains are washed as clean as in Philadelphia. Clothes and trunks grow moldy. Shoes removed at night are covered with green in the morning. You seem to grow moldy yourself. The entire system becomes relaxed, and great care needs to be exercised in the selection of food and drink. Then, when one's powers of resistance seem almost exhausted, the sun bursts forth with mid-summer force, and the thermometer ranges up to a limit of perhaps 90 degrees, Fahrenheit. Everything goes out upon the line to dry. One's spirits revive. Ungainly pith hats come out, for the westerner in Korea, as in so many other localities in the Orient, must protect the head against the direct rays of the sun. Mosquitoes and bull-frogs make the nights melodious; then, after a few days of glorious sunshine, the rains commence again. The rainy season proper begins with July 1st and ends the 15th of August; but not infrequently it lasts from late June to early September, a period of three months. At its close quinine becomes a table relish to ward off malaria.

But if the rainy season is trying, it would be a national calamity to be without it, for the rice ponds, to which the nation looks for the main staple in its year's supply of food, are carefully banked and terraced so as to drain from one into the other, and wait for the poured-out blessing of rain to bring the golden harvest. If the Koreans could not live without rice, quite as little could they do without rice straw. With it the common people prepare the feed for their stock, thatch their roofs, make their sandals, braid ropes, weave cables for the anchors of their junks, make sails and the mats for their floors, tie up their strings of ten eggs each, and make the sprawling images of men filled with small coin which they throw upon the roadside the fifteenth day of the first moon of the year to carry away their ill-luck. Korean rice is of a good quality, and much of it is shipped to Japan. When the rice supply grows scanty, in the late spring, the country people boil barley in its stead for their main food staple. Millet is similarly used in some localities. Wheat is used almost exclusively in making liquor. From buckwheat they make a kind of vermicelli, out of which they prepare a dish called "cook-su," of which foreigners are very fond. Beans are used for food—put sparingly into the rice kettles, or decomposed for a peppery sauce which furnishes one of their side dishes. Again, they are mixed with chopped straw and boiled in water, forming a hot mixture that is the sole food of the cattle and horses of Korea. Beans are also an article of export. A species of turnip or enormous white radish called "mu" is used in a sliced form for another of the side dishes which they eat with their rice. Another product is the "paichu," a species of cabbage shaped something like a nubbin of corn. This, with the red pepper—which, spread out to dry in the fall on the farmer's thatched roof, adds such a touch of color to the rural scenery—is used with other ingredients for making a species of sauerkraut, of which the Koreans are fond. Most Korean side dishes, I may remark, are seasoned very highly with either salt or red pepper, or cooked with vegetable oil. Ginger, onions and lettuce are grown in their gardens. There is a very limited production of potatoes. Tobacco is raised in large quantities. Broom corn and hemp are also cultivated. Cotton also grows in their fields. It may be mentioned parenthetically that most of the clothing worn by Koreans is made out of cotton cloth, part of which is native and part the product of the looms of Osaka and Manchester. Silk goods are also woven, for which industry the mulberry tree and the silkworm are cultivated. The ginseng root, so highly prized as a medicine in China, is grown as a government monopoly. Korea is essentially an agricultural country, with methods of cultivation that are crude, yet effective. The farmers all live in villages. Large tracts of land lie untilled.

There is considerable mineral wealth in the country. Iron in the forms of limonite and magnetic ore is profitably mined. An excellent quality of anthracite coal comes from the vicinity of Pyeng-yang. Tin, copper, lead and silver mines exist. Gold in considerable quantities is carried out of the country each year, part of which sees the custom-house, and probably as much more which does not is exported to China and Japan.   One hundred miles north from Pyeng-yang, at Unsan, gold is being mined by an American syndicate, which also has under construction the first railroad to be built in Korea, which will run from Chemulpo to Seoul.

In the matter of fruits there is first a woody pear, which reminds me of the remark of my lamented friend Ritchie, of China, in speaking of similar fruit in that country: "It all depends on what you are eating it for.   If you are eating it for a turnip, it is very good."   There are musk-melons, apricots, nectarines, grapes, a small red cherry that grows on a bush, scrubby apples, luscious persimmons and excellent chestnuts and walnuts.   The Koreans have fine-looking cattle which they use, bullocks and cows alike, for working in the fields, carrying loads and dragging great clumsy carts.   Cowhide is an article of export.   Koreans never think of drinking milk, and express great disrelish for the taste of but-ter.   The average Korean is too poor to eat beef and pork with any regularity, and in their stead he eats various varieties of fish, and, though he is slow to admit it to the foreigner, he occasionally roasts his dog.   A few sheep exist, which are reserved as sacred animals for royal sacrifice to Hananim, on special occasions, such as a drouth.

The Korean pony is small, sure-footed, pos-

sessed of great endurance, but frequently vicious.
It is used as a beast of burden, and shares with
the aristocrat's donkey the honor of use under the
saddle. For an appreciative description of the
Korean pony I commend you to Rev. J. S. Gale's
sketch in the Korean *Repository*.

Every house keeps a wolfish or currish dog,
brave to a fault—in barking. Cats exist and
razor-backed pigs. There are also rats, mice, and
weasels. If one knows where to go, where
mountains are many and men are few, tigers,
leopards, foxes, wild boar, and deer can be found
in the country. Saucy magpies, screaming kites,
inky crows and armies of sparrows are to be seen
everywhere. In the country may be heard the
cuckoo's and the wild pigeon's notes; and the lark
pours forth his melody. The stately stork and
crane swoop over the rice fields. Falcons and
eagles are seen rarely. Many a pheasant starts
up from beside the country road, resplendent in
the gorgeous plumage that finds a faint reflection
in the markings of the barn-yard fowls, so plentiful in Korea. Near the seashore a tree top is
visible now and then, filled with the nests of the
noisy blue heron. The graceful swan is seen
occasionally; and wild ducks and geese abound,
plentiful enough to stir the huntsman's heart.

This sketchy view of the nature of the country
and its products may serve as a canvas upon
which we may throw, in the pages that follow,
our pictures of life in Korea.

CHAPTER II

As the beginnings of Grecian history are inextricably intertwined with the loves and jealousies of the gods, and English history has its early legends of the marvels of King Arthur's court, so the history of Korea is sufficiently old to lose itself in mythical traditions. Mystery has always enveloped the Ever-White Mountains on the northern frontier of the land. The people in the olden time, according to tradition, lived without a ruler, until a deity descended from heaven and made his home at the foot of a sandal-tree upon the Ever-White Mountains. The people, recognizing his superiority, made him their king and called him Dan-Kun, or the "Sandal Prince." He made his earliest home in Pyeng-yang, where to this day there is a temple to his honor, and his descendants are said to have reigned for a thousand years. However, Chinese and Korean tradition alike affirm that a being somewhat more authentic, the Chinese noble, Keja, was the founder of the social order of Korea. Keja lived in the days of the wicked emperor Chow Sin, the "Nero of China." He was one of three wise counselors who met with the usual fate of the givers of good advice to wicked kings. One was killed, one had to flee, and the third was locked up in prison, the last-mentioned being Keja. But a usurper rid the country of the tyrant, and himself ascended the throne. The new king would gladly have given to Keja the highest office in the state, but the latter seems to have had as painful a conscience as any non-juring rector in the days of King William of Orange; and he declared that his duty to the dead king forbade him taking office under one whom he considered a usurper. Another case, you see, of the "divine right of kings." The upshot of the matter was that Keja, gathering together a band of several thousand retainers, the remnants of the defeated army, in the year 1122 B. C., while Samuel was still a judge at the other end of the continent, went into voluntary exile and settled among the aborigines of Korea. He gave to his kingdom the name of Chosen, which, be it noted, is the modern native name for Korea. He vigorously carried forward the work, said to have been begun by the mythical Dan Kun, of giving to the country a civilization such as he had known in China, his sphere of influence being Southern Manchuria and Northern Korea, between the rivers Liao and Tatong. The city of Pyeng-yang is said to contain his grave; and in two of the largest cities of the country, Pyeng-yang in the north and Chun-ju in the south, I have seen large temples that were erected in his honor. Tradition also states that the descendants of Keja reigned as kings over what has been known as Ancient Chosen.

The historical muse now apparently suffered from a long lapse of memory; for it is not until some two hundred years before Christ that the narrative is resumed.   Tradition from this period is replaced by a detailed record.   Of Korea's ancient history I shall give, in the briefest manner only, an outline of important events and changes that have been made in the map.   These are culled from the many scores of pages in which Dr. W. E. Griffis, with infinite research, has chronicled in his "Corea, the Hermit Nation," the history of the country until the era of the treaties, some fifteen years ago.   The central location of Korea, a peacefully inclined country with warlike nations to the west, north and east, has made its history largely a record of invasions from China, Mongolia, and Japan.   The invaders would come on their conquering career, and the people would bend for a time like forest trees before the storm.   But, the pressure being removed, they would resume their national life.; a nominal tribute would be paid for a term of years, then after a time they would forget they ever had been conquered, when another tidal wave of war would pour over them from without.

The Koreans never have shown great valor in the fighting of pitched battles, but it has been rather in irregular warfare and as garrison fighters that they have been most successful.   It was about 107 B. C. that Ancient Chosen, in which was embraced the four northern provinces of Korea, North and South Pyeng An and North and South Ham Kyeng, finally fell before the armies of the Han dynasty, and for a century or two came under the sway of China.

The destinies of these northern sections of Korea were presently to become affected by the incoming of a people from still farther north. The Fuyu race had their home in northern Manchuria, near the Sungari River. In comparison with the surrounding peoples they had a singularly high order of civilization. From Fuyu migrated southward what became the Kokorio tribes, whose seat was to the north and west of the headwaters of the Yalu, near the Ever-White Mountains. About 70 A. D. they began to enlarge their borders till they absorbed the north of Korea and came into collision with the Chinese, whose power they displaced as far as the limits of Liao Tung, in Manchuria, which was known thereafter as the country of Korio. They sustained, until the seventh century, a fitful warfare with the Chinese, who had troubles in their own land, so that, although they sent an occasional invading army, they could never give the continuous attention to these eastern tribes which was needed in order to subdue them.

Let us consider next the early history of Southern Korea, which for present purposes we may consider to be all the territory lying south of the Tatong

River. At the time Ancient Chosen was absorbed into China, in 107 B. C., all Southern Korea was divided into three *Han* or geographical divisions, the Mahan in the western central part, the Benhan in the south, and the Shinhan in the eastern central portion of the peninsula. These were loosely joined confederacies of aboriginal tribes, with spirit worship for their only religion, and with a rather low grade of civilization, though it should be mentioned that relatively the Shinhan people were of a much higher order, for they lived in palisaded cities and had already learned the art of weaving silk and working iron. It is stated that in the first century A. D. works of skill and art were sent from here to the Mikado of Japan which were greatly superior to anything produced in the Island Empire of that day. Probably the secret of their advanced state is that refugees from China had settled in their midst. But certain political changes are to be noted. Kijun, a king deposed in old Chosen, fled southward, and among the Mahan tribes set up what is known among the Koreans as the Pakje, and among the Japanese writers as the Hiaksai Kingdom. The name Shinhan became changed to the Silla Kingdom.

Inter-tribal war was of frequent occurrence, and presently the map of all Korea would need readjustment as follows: There are now three kingdoms—Korio in the north, Silla in the southeast and Pakje in the southwest of the peninsula.

We are now in the epoch of the three kingdoms. The kingdom of Pakje presently became the leading state. Here, in 374 A. D., the writings of Confucius and Mencius first entered the peninsula from China. A decade later Buddhism likewise established itself in Pakje. In the following century the men of Pakje, having defeated an invading army from China, their independence was virtually recognized by the emperor. About 660, in the course of their internal warfare, Silla appealed to China for aid, which was granted, and as the result of the war Pakje became absorbed into China. But presently they were again in arms, and invoked the aid of Japan against Silla. The Japanese sent a fleet, which, however, was surprised and sunk by the allied armies of China and Silla, with the result that the kingdom of Pakje was utterly laid waste. Large bodies of the people of Pakje, about 700 A. D., emigrated to Japan, introducing, it is supposed, the study of the writings of Gautama and of the great sage of China. Let us turn once more to the kingdom of Korio in the north. The government of Korio was feudal, with great nobles almost as powerful as the king. In 641 one of these murdered the king and seized the throne. The Chinese emperor acknowledged his sovereignty, but ordered him to cease the invasion of Silla, China's ally. He refused and a great invading army came by sea and land from China. By the splendid defense of the city of An-ju the men

of Korio held their own till the Chinese, from lack
of provisions, had to withdraw, and, like the fate
of Napoleon's army in the Moscow campaign,
thousands of Chinese soldiers died in the winter
retreat. In 664, however, another invasion was
more successful, and the kingdom of Korio disappeared from the map.

Let us turn our attention next to the kingdom
of Silla. The island of Kiushiu, upon which is
located the modern city of Nagasaki, brought
this kingdom into early collision with Japan; for
settlers from Silla came to believe that they
owned the island, which opinion was disputed by
the men of the dominant Yamato tribe, living in
the vicinity of Kioto. The result was that in 200
A. D. the Japanese, under Queen Jingu, marched
to suppress the so-called Kiushiu "rebels."
Being convinced that the root of the trouble lay
in the peninsula, the queen crossed with her army
to the mainland, overran without resistance the
kingdom of Silla, and returned to Japan with rich
tribute. From this time may be said to have originated the claim of Japan, so similar to that of
China, that Korea was their tributary country.

Intermittent war was waged between the men
of Silla and the allied forces of Pakje and Korio
down to the tenth century, in which occasionally
the Japanese would assist Pakje, or the Chinese
would be allied with Silla, or the nations north of
the peninsula would help Korio. Buddhism,
introduced into the kingdom in 528, steadily

grew to be the prevailing religion.   One of the
ablest scholars of Silla is credited with the
invention of the admirable native alphabet, to be
mentioned later.   Kiong-ju, the capital of the
kingdom, developed into a city of great relative
material splendor and a center of learning and
refinement whose influence was felt, not only
throughout all Korea, but as far as the court of
Japan, teaching the arts of peace.   Politically,
Silla finally came to rule the entire eastern half
of the peninsula, until, as the last of the three
kingdoms, she fell, in 934, to give place to united
Korea.

In speaking now of united Korea, we need to
notice that sometime in the ninth century, race
movements north of the Tumen River brought
into Northern Korea large numbers of emigrants,
who soon grew prosperous.   Out of these people
a Buddhist monk named Kung-wo, in 912, raised
an army under the flag of rebellion; but he was
presently killed and succeeded by his lieutenant,
Wang, a descendant of the old royal house of
Korio.   China was at that time occupied with wars
at home.   Moreover, the government of Silla, the
one remaining kingdom, had grown decrepit.
Thus Wang had everything his own way and a
very few years sufficed to bring the entire
peninsula under his sway.   He chose for the
site of his capital the city of Song-do, also known
as Kai-seng, some sixty miles northwest of Seoul.
Here his descendants reigned for four hundred

years.   For convenience we may think of this
period of history as the era of the Song-do
dynasty.   The kingdom took the name of Korio.
This was the golden age of Korean Buddhism.
Wang's son and successor speedily formed an
alliance with China, and sent her tribute.   One
hundred years before the time of Gutenberg the
Koreans were printing books from wooden blocks,
whence the art was introduced into Japan.

Genghis Khan, the Alexander of the Orient,
who with his Mongol hard riders conquered nearly
the whole of Asia, sent one of his three armies to
conquer Korea and Japan.   In 1218 the Korean
king declared himself the vassal of the great
Mongol chief.   A few years later a Mongol
envoy was murdered in Korea.   In answer, an
invading army came, which divided the country
under Mongol prefects.   The people, as soon as
they dared, rose and murdered them all.   Then
they were invaded in earnest, and, among other
exactions, the Korean king was required to do
homage in person at the conqueror's court.   For
several decades, though always turbulent, the
Koreans were held under Mongol rule.   Kublai
Khan, the grandson of Genghis, in 1281 forced
the Koreans to assist in an unsuccessful invasion
of Japan.   Their presence among the invaders
helped to intensify the hatred between the penin-
sular kingdom and the island empire.   From this
time, for two or three centuries, the Japanese
central government being weakened through the

prevalence of civil wars, Japanese pirates were abundant, who drove Korean junks from the seas and made the life of coast dwellers miserable. This did not improve the state of feeling in Korea.

In 1392 there was a change of dynasties which brought to the front the Ye dynasty, now on the throne of Korea, though the direct line came to an end in 1864. The name of the country was also changed from Korio to the ancient term, Chosen. The Wang dynasty had greatly degenerated, and a tyrant was on the throne. Ye Taijo, a military officer, had risen to be the head of the army and had become the king's son-in-law. Korea for some time had neglected to send tribute to the Mongol ruler on the Dragon throne. The Mongols had made a half-hearted effort to again subdue Korea, but the troops under Ye Taijo repelled them. And now a Ming emperor was on the throne of China, who demanded pledges of vassalage, which the king, against the wishes of his people, refused to send. As Korea was about to be overwhelmed by the Ming veterans, Ye Taijo seized the reins of power, deposed the king and made his peace with the emperor. With Ye Taijo began the new dynasty, whose capital city was changed to its present location at Seoul. The dress and top-knot of the Ming era of China was at that time adopted in Korea, and continues in vogue to this day.

Tribute was sent to China and at first to Japan, though later it was discontinued. Japanese pirates, with Korean renegades for pilots, still harassed the coasts of Korea. But within the peninsula life grew easy. The people traded and tilled the fields. The officials and the military officers led a life of pleasure, and war was the last thing in the world for which they were prepared. Like a summer holiday, the time glided by until the close of the sixteenth century. Then came the two terrible Japanese invasions, like the sweep of a great tidal wave, leaving death and ruin behind them and the memory of dreadful deeds.

In 1585 a master general, Hideyoshi, had arisen in Japan, where for two centuries anarchy had reigned. His conquering hosts had brought the entire group of islands under the Mikado's feudal rule, and now waited on their arms for new foes to conquer. He had been given the highest rank attainable by a subject, and he was incensed that the Koreans, whom he regarded a tributary people, had failed to send their greetings with those of other vassals. He sent as envoy a tactless old warrior, to inquire why tribute of late years had ceased to be sent. His mission was a failure, and the old man lost his life on his return. Another envoy was more successful, and he returned with a tribute-bearing embassy from Korea. These, after a long delay, were granted an interview by Hideyoshi, and later he sent them, together with various presents, an insolent reply addressed to their king. He also sent asking the rulers of Korea to help them renew peaceful rela-

tions with China, which the pirates had disturbed.
The reply from Korea was naturally unsatisfac-
tory.   He then resolved not only to humble
China, but incidentally to crush Korea.   This
was in 1592.   The army which disembarked at
Fusan was enormous, well-provisioned, and con-
tained a corps trained in the use of match-lock
guns, a weapon at that time new to the East.   The
command of the troops was divided between two
generals; one, Konishi, an impetuous young man
and a Roman Catholic; the other, Kato, a fierce
old fighter and an ardent Buddhist.   Each was a
good leader in his way, but intensely jealous of
the other.   Konishi arrived first.   The fortress at
Tongnai, close to Fusan, quickly fell.   He at
once started north through the peninsula, following the course of the Naktong River as far as
Sang-ju.   Kato arrived a day later, and he fumed
with rage to learn that his rival had already taken
his departure.   He took the more western road,
sending detachments into the Chulla and Chung-
chong provinces.   Then began a race between
the rival armies to reach Seoul.   From Sang-
ju, in the Kiung-sang province, Konishi pushed
on to Chiong-ju in the Chung-chong province
and quickly reduced the city.   Kato arrived
here a few days later, but he redoubled his
energies, so that the very day Konishi entered
Seoul by one gate, he entered by another.   They
found a deserted city.   The king and his court,
accustomed to spend their days under the spell

of the flowing bowl and the attractions of dancing-girls, had found themselves unequal to the situation and had fled precipitately to Pyeng-yang in the north, amidst the drenching showers of the rainy season. Soldiers and people vied with each other in the speed of their flight to the mountains. The king had ordered the remnants of his army to make a stand at the Rim-chin River. Kato and Konishi, after a few days' rest in the empty capital, with united forces started north. At the Rim-chin River, by a feigned retreat, they induced the Koreans to cross, then routed them and seized their junks. Here the two Japanese leaders, owing to mutual jealousy, drew lots and parted company. Kato went to the eastern side, while Konishi remained on the western side of the peninsula, both of them headed for the north. Konishi marched on Pyeng-yang, while the king fled across the border at Eui-ju. Konishi camped upon the opposite side of the Tatong River till the Pyeng-yang troops made an unsuccessful night attack upon him, which only resulted in betraying the locations of the fords in the river to the Japanese, who, promptly availing themselves of the information, crossed and took the city. Here Konishi, before starting for China, awaited the arrival of his fleet, which, however, was never to come. Some Koreans had in the meantime been thinking and had evolved a new model of fighting-junk. With these they lured the Japanese fleet into the open sea and proceeded to demolish it. This greatly raised the spirits of the Koreans, who had hitherto seemed dazed by the rapidity and success of the Japanese movements. The king, from Liao Tung, was sending importunate appeals for help to the court of Peking. A few thousand Chinese troops marched down from Liao Tung into Korea. The Japanese allowed them to enter the streets of the city of Pyeng-yang, and then, from well-chosen positions, attacked and cut them to pieces. The court of Peking now took the invasion seriously. They began at once to raise an army of 40,000 men, and juggled with characteristic Chinese diplomacy in order to gain time. About all of importance that Kato had done in the meanwhile was to capture a couple of Korean royal princes. Koreans were beginning to organize bands for guerrilla warfare. In 1593 came the Chinese army, 60,000 strong, and aided by Korean troops attacked for two days the fortifications the Japanese had reared on the hills north of the city of Pyeng-yang. Then Konishi withdrew his troops in the night, and retreated to Seoul. Small Japanese garrisons were being taken by Korean bands. Kato presently yielded to the appeals of his colleague, and also returned to Seoul. The allies now began to advance on the capital. Then came the terrible massacre in which the Japanese troops put to the sword hundreds of non-combatants, drove out others and laid waste large portions of the city. Later a

terrific battle was fought near Seoul, in which
the allied Chinese and Korean troops were worsted
and withdrew to Song-do.

A winter of suffering from famine and pestilence
in an exhausted country settled down.   At its
close a treaty of peace was concluded, and the
Japanese returned to Fusan.

While negotiations were pending the Japanese
showed that, while they were willing to be at
peace with China, they did not consider that
they were done with unhappy Korea.   Kato was
given orders to capture the walled city of Chin-ju
in Southeastern Korea.   I have seen in that city
the temple built in honor of a Korean dancing-
girl who at this period is said to have lured on
shore a Japanese general and then drowned herself and him at the same time from a flat rock in
the river.   After a most stubborn resistance on
the part of the Koreans the city was taken and
large   numbers   of   people   were   put   to   the
sword.

Hideyoshi, considering himself insulted by the
form of address in the letter of the Chinese
emperor, sent with an embassy, broke off negotiations and renewed the war in what is known as
the second invasion of Korea.   A Chinese army
marched down to the city of Nam-cung, in South-
western Korea.   The first battle of the campaign
was a naval one off the southern coast of the
country, in which the Korean fleet came to grief.
Kato and Konishi now moved on Nam-cung, with

its splendid walls. After some days' fighting the walls were scaled by piling up bundles of green rice on one side and by climbing a secret mountain path on the other. In the fight which ensued thousands of Koreans and Chinese were slain, whose noses and ears were later cut off and shipped to Japan to form the great "ear mound," now to be seen under its monument in Kioto.

About the same time, off the south coast of Korea, the Chinese and Japanese fleets fought a battle, in which the fleet of the latter was annihilated. This, as in the other invasion, really defeated the Japanese, as it destroyed the supply of food upon which they relied. The Japanese advanced almost to Seoul, but learning of the approach of large reinforcements for the Chinese army, and their food supply growing scanty, they began their retreat, spoiling the houses and temples as they went of everything of value. This was notably true of the ancient and magnificent city of Kiong-ju, once the capital of Silla, which they not only spoiled, but burned to the ground.

They finally rested within the fortifications of Ulsan, where part of them remained. This place was besieged by an army of the allies, and much desperate fighting followed. The siege was finally raised owing to Japanese successes elsewhere, and more noses and ears were sent to Japan. For a time the war lingered on. Then Hideyoshi died and the Japanese troops were recalled. This ended the terrible war. Tribute was sent for a hundred years or so, and then its sending was discontinued.

Life passed comparatively uneventful in the peninsula until the regions to the north sent forth another host of hard riders in the Manchus. In 1619 the Koreans, who had at first helped the Chinese, became convinced that the Manchus were destined to triumph—which they did eventually, and seated one of their number on the Dragon throne—so they went over to the Manchus. But they continued to give real assistance to the Chinese. Presently the Manchus found time to turn their attention to the Koreans, and twice invaded the country as far as Seoul, leaving death and destruction behind them. The king and his court in each case fled down the Han River to the island of Kang-wha, which was captured in the second invasion. The king had now to make his allegiance actual by furnishing the Manchus with grain and providing them with a small army. To the new Manchu emperor they also had to send yearly a stipulated tribute; such, for instance, as 100 ounces of gold, 10,000 bags of rice, 100 tiger skins, etc.

Thence until the recent past they saw no more of invading armies. In 1653 a Dutch ship was wrecked off Quelpart Island and the men were held as slaves in the peninsula for a number of years. One of their number, Hamil, escaped and wrote a book upon the country. At the close of the last century a Chinese priest, and in 1835 French fathers of the Jesuit order of Roman Catholics, slipped secretly, at the risk of their lives, into the peninsula, to follow up work which had germinated from the reading of some religious tracts that had found their way into the country from China.   The account of their labors and sufferings is admirably told in Dallet's "Histoire de l'Eglise de Corée."

The revolutionary nature, from a Korean point of view, of the new teachings, which demanded nothing less than the abandonment of their most sacred custom, the worship of ancestors, together with the discovery of what they considered treasonable political intrigue in a letter written by a Korean convert inviting the invasion of western armies, early brought upon the Catholic adherents murderous persecution.   In 1839 three French fathers were killed.   And in the minority of the present king (while the cruel Tai-won-kun, his father, was on the throne as regent), occurred the terrible martyrdoms of 1866.   Fear of foreign aggression and the rumor that the Chinese were killing the Catholic adherents in their country were the inciting causes.   Fourteen bishops and priests, with thousands of their Korean converts, suffered martyrdom.

In reprisal, in the following year, a French fleet appeared off the coast; but nothing came of the expedition beyond a brush with the Korean soldiers guarding the island of Kang-wha, in the

Han River. In 1871 came some American gun-boats to avenge the murder of the crew of the American schooner "Gen. Sherman," wrecked near Pyeng-yang, and after brisk fighting the men of the "Monocacy" and "Palos" captured five forts on the island of Kang-wha. In 1876, the present king now reigning in his own right, a treaty was signed between Korea and Japan which opened the long-closed gates of the "Her-mit Kingdom." With the help of Li Hung Chang, Admiral Schufeldt, in 1882, secured a treaty between Korea and the United States, and treaties with other western nations followed. Before the year closed a reactionary insurrection, incited by the foreign-hating Tai-won-kun, took place, in which a number of Japanese were killed and Tai-won-kun was kidnaped by a Chinese warship and taken to China. China—although before the signing of the treaties, when the murders of the French fathers and the crew of the "Gen Sherman" were under discussion—had declared that she was in no wise responsible for the Korean government, yet later she made much of the fact that yearly tribute had been sent to her, and her "Resident," by subtle diplomacy, made himself the power behind the throne, at least in checking all progress along western lines. Judge O. N. Denny of Oregon, for several years adviser to his majesty, although appointed through the influence of Li Hung Chang, felt it his duty to strongly combat the position assumed by

China. A party of progressive young nobles, rendered desperate by conservative opposition, organized the "emeute of 1884." High officials were killed. For three days the young nobles ruled the kingdom. Then Chinese soldiers appeared in opposition, and Japanese soldiers took the part of the young men. There was fighting, and the young men had to flee, some to Japan and some to the United States, while the Japanese, with their citizens in a hollow square, fought their way down to the coast. Chinese influence now had a clear field.

The Chino-Japanese war of 1894 is so recent that few comments are necessary. An insurrection having occurred in the south of the country, due to excessive extortion upon the part of the officials, the king of Korea asked the help of Chinese troops, who were sent by Li Hung Chang. This the Japanese resented as contrary to the Chino-Japanese treaty, which allowed only a legation guard of Chinese in the country. The Japanese came with the rallying cry, "The independence of Korea," drove the Chinese out of the country, and took the two great forts that guard the entrance from the sea to the Korean capital. The main events of the war were the sinking of the Chinese transport ship, "Kowshing," bearing the British flag, the land battles in Korea at Asan and Pyeng-yang, the naval fight off the mouth of the Yalu, and the taking of the Chinese fortresses at Port Arthur and Wei-hai-wei. Incidentally, the Japanese stormed the Korean palace and revolutionized the government, putting into the government offices Koreans favorable to their schemes of reform. Granted the right of Japan, which was not conceded at the time by the representatives of the other nations, to march her armies into the land of a friendly country and overturn its government, the reforms instituted by the Japanese were in the main most excellent. And that they made an honest effort to carry them out was seen in their sending as minister Count Inouye, one of the best administrators in their country. Then came the blunder of the Ito cabinet, so fatal to Japanese interests, in the sending of Viscount Miura as his successor, followed by the dreadful murder, October 8, 1895, of the queen, known to have been by far the most astute politician in Korea. For months the grief-stricken king was held a close prisoner in his own palace. Then one bright morning, in February of the following year, by a clever ruse his majesty and the crown prince slipped out of the palace in the closed chairs of palace ladies, and fled for refuge to the Russian legation. There they met with a cordial welcome from the Russian minister, Mr. Waeber, and his gracious wife, who have moved recently to their new diplomatic home in Mexico City, and both of whom, I may remark in passing, were highly respected and beloved by all the foreigners in Korea. From that time onward the influence of the Great

Northern Empire has steadily increased in the peninsula.* At the Russian legation his majesty remained for a year, and then moved to his new palace within the foreign settlement. It is understood that this autumn he will assume the title of emperor, and that the name of the country will be changed from Chosen, the "land of morning calm," to that of Daihan, whose significance is that of "Great Han," Han being the term which, as will be remembered, was applied to each of the political divisions of the land in the dawn of its history.

---

* As the book goes to press, word has come that the Russians have reversed their policy in Korea. They have recalled the thirteen military instructors and the financial adviser, who but a short time previous had displaced Dr. J. McLeavey Brown, and have entered into a compact with the Japanese in which it is mutually agreed that neither country shall nominate military instructors nor financial advisers for Korea without a prior agreement between the two contracting powers.

CHAPTER III

How well I remember the afternoon our steamer swung around Deer Island, where the Russians have been trying to get a coaling-station, into the round harbor of Fusan, disclosing the strange, new land to our unaccustomed eyes. I can see now the green-covered hills, with here and there a white object stalking over their surface that suggested only too distinctly the beings that are said to creep in church-yards after the night has fallen. Koreans almost universally dress in white, and the fashion of their garments is unique. Let us study the attire of my friend, Mr. Pak, as he sits near by all unconsciously puffing away at his long-stemmed pipe; for the smoking of tobacco is common among the men and women of Korea. On his head is a round, tapering, flat-topped hat, with a brim thirteen inches in diameter, woven with very fine strips of bamboo, which make it exceedingly light. This hat is ordinarily black in color, but under certain circumstances the mourning customs of the country require it to be of a whitish-yellow hue. Except in the seclusion of his home this hat is always upon his head. As he slips the ribbon from under his chin and removes the hat for a moment, we see that his hair is done up in a very peculiar way. He has suffered the coarse black locks to grow very long, and, I may remark, periodically has a large square tonsure shaven on the top of his head; but this you would never guess as you look at him, for his hair has been gathered up and tightly coiled in a top-knot, two or three inches long and a single inch in diameter, which stands straight up from the crown of his head. Bound about his brow, so tightly as to cause a slight depression in the forehead, is a band of woven horsehair, two inches wide. This serves to hold his hair in place and into it he occasionally tucks a straggling lock with a tool that looks like a little horn paper-knife.

As Mr. Pak considers himself rather a gentleman, should you see him in the seclusion of his home you would observe on his head a skullcap of black horse hair, dented in at the front so that it looks like a two-stepped horse block; or again, either with or without this skullcap, you might see on him another style of horse-hair hat that gives one something of the impression of a royal crown that had been flattened under a letter-press. Think of a suit of clothes without a single button! Everything is tied up with a girdle or with some form of band with one end sewed to the cloth. Mr. Pak wears next his body a jacket reaching to the waist; and over this, while away from home, he wears a full-sleeved loose robe that falls to his ankles. Beneath it you catch an occasional glimpse of a pouch or two, and of the case for his scholarly goggles hanging from the trousers girdle. The trousers themselves are baggy and are gathered in below the knees with a pair of cloth leggings tied at the ankles. He wears a pair of stockings padded with cotton batting. On his feet are a pair of felt sandals which he leaves out of doors whenever he enters a house. This is the picture which Mr. Pak presents. In the winter he wears clothes padded with cotton, including an overcoat, and clinging to the sides of his head a black fur-edged covering that keeps his ears warm. Here and there you see a man with a coat dyed some shade of blue or green; or a black coat showing white sleeves. Silk garments are seen occasionally. The laboring classes frequently wear for a coat only the short jacket; their working trousers fit more closely and their feet are shod with sandals of straw or twine. Koreans sometimes wear leather sandals and, in muddy weather, you will see wooden shoes raised by a couple of bits of wood three inches above the ground. On the chair-coolie's head you will see a round-crowned, wide-brimmed, black felt hat. Yonder farmer, following his ox laden with a towering mass of brush for firewood, wears on his head a convex arrangement, two feet in diameter, of coarsely-woven thin strips of wood which, in shape, looks something like the top of a circus tent.

Of the Koreans it may be said that, while sharing in many of the characteristics of the other

IRONING CLOTHES.

inhabitants of the Far East, racially they are a type by themselves. In height they average fairly well with the people of Northern China. The Korean face will bear study. The forehead, sufficiently high, shows no lack of brains. The bright black eyes are slightly almond-pinched at the corners. The nose is rather low and flat, and the lips are full. Another type of features, it may be remarked, is also frequently seen, especially in the north of the country, in which the eyes are round and the features are regular, sometimes even delicately chiseled; but the black hair and black eyes are practically universal. Mr. Pak wears a thin mustache and a few straggling hairs adorn his chin—no need for him to shave every day, for the simple reason that the Koreans, with few exceptions, have nothing or almost nothing on their faces to require the use of a razor.

The Korean houses are peculiar. Generically they may be divided into two classes—those roofed with a deep thatch of rice straw, seen almost universally in the country villages, and those covered with a black-tiled roof, usually on the homes of the well-to-do. With the exception of a very few government and business buildings the houses are all one-story structures. The framework of a Korean roof is so cleverly mortised together that not a nail is required in its construction. In the support of this framework, with its burden of thatch, or tiles set in loose earth, well-planed logs of wood cross the rooms overhead, and these rest in turn on wooden pillars erected at intervals of eight feet. The tiled roofs are gracefully curved upward at the corners, and both varieties of roof project three or four feet beyond the building proper. In the construction of the walls a wicker work of twigs is woven, and over this mud is plastered, making an adobe wall, which, however, is occasionally faced with stone. The windows are double. The outside ones are latticed and swing on rude hinges, while the inner ones slide in grooves, and both sets are covered with tough paper that admits a dim light, though inserted in them may occasionally be seen a single pane or bit of glass. In making their floors the Koreans have hit upon quite an economical mode of heating their rooms, although it is death to ventilation. By the use of stone and mud, perhaps six parallel flues are built up, which converge at each end into an opening leading outside, one into the chimney, the other into the fireplace. These flues are covered over with matched stone slabs, and a smooth coating of mud is laid over all. When this has been well dried, in many cases two layers of paper, of which the upper one is thick and well saturated with oil, are neatly pasted over the floor. The walls and ceiling of the room may or may not be covered with wall-paper, generally white. At least one room has its fireplace so constructed that a couple of round, shallow iron kettles for boiling rice or heating water may be fastened into them. For

fuel they burn chopped wood, pine brush or hay.
In cool weather a dish of coals is always in evidence to warm the hands and to light the pipes. I
have had some experience with Korean floors. In
my country trips, following the native custom, at
night I simply spread my sleeping arrangements
on the floor, well sprinkled, however, with "insect
powder." In a Korean's case, let me remark,
they would consist of a small wooden block for
a pillow, a quilt, and possibly a thin mattress.
If in a room where the amount of fuel used in
heating the stones under you can be regulated,
you experience only a genial glow running up
and down your spine; but take the case of a Korean inn where under you rolls the fire used to cook
the food of a dozen men, and you feel like a trout
in the skillet. In whatever other ways Korean
houses differ, one feature they have in common—
there is always a square or rectangular inner
court, carefully shielded from the gaze of the
public by buildings and high walls. Within this
court are jars of food and a little bed of flowers.
The living-rooms are generally on two sides of the
court. There is the black, smoke-stained kitchen,
containing the fireplace with the iron pots mentioned above. Here are also cooking utensils,
and yonder, not unlikely, bundles of fuel piled upon
the floor of earth. Next to this is a sleeping and
living room, possibly capable of subdivision with
sliding, paper-covered doors. At right angles to
this sleeping-room is a wide, enclosed porch with

a wooden floor, completely open on the side of the court.   Here the bowls of crockery or brass are stored in brass-trimmed cupboards and the dining-tables are stacked, and here the women, in suitable weather, pass the most of their monotonous existence, seated upon the well-polished floor, for chairs are not used by Koreans.   Indeed, the only other article of furniture seen is an occasional painted or embroidered screen or chest more or less decorated, or possibly a greasy lampstand holding the little bowl of vegetable oil with a bit of wick resting on the edge.   Some, however, especially in the ports, use little kerosene lamps.   Then on the other side of the porch will be another living-room with flues under the floor.   Next the kitchen, or on the third side of the court will be a shed or two, with native locks and ring-and-staple fastenings on the doors.   On the fourth side is the "sarang," a room with openings outside, where the male friends of the man of the house congregate, with never a thought of venturing in to see the ladies of the house.   Furthermore, it is not considered polite for the gentlemen to ask much about them. One curious fact is that in the country none but members of the aristocratic class are allowed to have little verandas on the outside of their sarangs.

Dinner is announced, and the little square or round tables, twelve inches high, are found steaming in the porch of the inner quarters, or if friends

of the host are out in the "sarang" two or three
laden tables will be passed in for them at a
window. Everyone gets down upon the floor
in the usual Korean sitting posture, cross-legged
like a tailor, sometimes one and sometimes two
at a table. The first course, if the occasion be an
especial one, is a bowl of soup. The heaping
bowl of rice is then discussed, either with the brass
spoon or chop sticks. And the chop-sticks de-
scend every now and then upon the contents of the
little side dishes, the brine-soaked "mu," or turnip,
the bits of dried fish or meats, a species of sauerkraut composed of cabbage, shrimp, ginger, onion,
red pepper, salt, etc., with an occasional dip into
the bean sauce (à la Worcestershire). For liquid
food he drinks cold water, or the water in which
the rice has been cooked. Poor people often eat
with their rice only the sauerkraut or pickled
turnip. Korean etiquette allows much smacking
of the lips while eating; but if dining out in the
sarang, in the presence of a visitor, politeness
requires him either to offer him food or excuse
himself for eating. Koreans also eat with the
rapidity of a traveler at a railway lunch counter,
or a table full of threshers.

Linguistically the Koreans are furnished with
a language that takes second place to neither
the Chinese nor Japanese languages in difficulty
of acquisition. The young Westerner entering
upon its mastery has just one thing in his favor—
he does not know what he is getting into. Three

modes of expression are in use among the Koreans—the colloquial, the book language and the
Chinese written characters.   Let us first notice
the colloquial—the language of the people—which,
when reduced to writing, is known as the
"Unmun."   The Unmun alphabet comprises
twenty-eight letters, which are combined in syl-
lables that are written one under the other in ver-
tical columns and are read from the back end to
the front of the book.   Korean scholars affect to
despise this style of writing, its use in former
years having been confined largely to the printing
of flashy novels, though of late its use in the
printing of   missionary literature and   certain
newspapers has helped to give it dignity.   Struc-
turally the colloquial may be termed agglutinative.
Many of the root forms are derived from the
Chinese.   The noun endings rival the Greek in
number, though used rather carelessly in ordinary
conversation.   The verbal endings mount into the
hundreds, and   prepositions, conjunctions and
endings that mean the same as our marks of
punctuation have a way of sticking to the root
formations.   One thing which multiplies the
number of verbal endings is the custom of the
country that gradations in age and social position
require a varying use of high, low and middle
forms.   A teacher in one of the girls' schools in
Seoul one day found two of her little girls in a
violent quarrel over the question of which should
use high language to the other.   "I am the

older," cried one; "I am the bigger," sobbed the other.

Second, the book language, after the manner of Latinized English, is largely composed of words derived from the Chinese. It is written in the Unmun character and is used in a few translations of the Chinese classics, in parallel sections with the orginal. It is also employed in certain other moral writings.

Third, in the Chinese characters the scholars read the literature of China, and do their letter writing. All government documents are written or printed in Chinese.

Speaking of gradations in social position, corresponding to the "literati" in China and the "samurai" in Japan, the Koreans have an aristocratic class know as "yangbans." They are the scholars, the possessors of blue blood, the holders of government offices. They are ardent Confucianists and are intensely conservative. Among their own class they are hospitable and punctiliously polite. The poor yangbans have a way of sponging upon their more fortunate relatives and friends. They let their finger-nails grow long to show their contempt for labor, and they despise the classes below them in the social scale. I saw a young man with a stone in his hand chase another man all over a village one night, because the latter, belonging to a lower social grade than he, had dared to smoke a pipe in his presence.

Slavery exists in a mild form in the country. For the most part slaves are attached to families as bond-servants, much as was the custom in Old Testament times. One class of slaves are men and are the hereditary property of rich nobles. In another class the women alone are counted as property, and can redeem themselves or secure their freedom by leaving in their place an able-bodied daughter in the state of bondage. A third class are the female slaves attached to magistracies—female criminals, or the wives of criminals. They are truly to be pitied, for their degradation passes description.

The government of Korea is an absolute monarchy. The king, however, calls to his assistance a council of state composed of a chancellor and various ministers and councilors. Certain of the departments have foreign advisers, two of whom, Dr. J. McLeavey Brown, adviser to the finance department, as well as chief commissioner of the customs service, and General C. G. Greathouse, the former U. S. Consul General at Yokohama and present adviser to the law department, have of late rendered distinguished service to the Korean Government. The Korean troops in Seoul are at present under the instruction of three commissioned and ten non-commissioned Russian officers. Each of the thirteen provinces has its governor, with a proper number of assistants; and each of the 339 magistracies in these provinces has its magistrate with a force of writers and runners. Every village has its head, generally an old man. Official honesty is apparently a thing almost unknown in Korea, and the poor people lead a sorry life; for not only must the regular taxes be paid, but they are subject to the further exactions of officials, runners, inspectors, policemen, soldiers, not to mention the bands of robbers that roam the country every winter and spring. Much of the so-called laziness of the Koreans is simply apathy, produced by the insecurity of property rights. With the exception of a few rich merchants and men who own large estates in the country, the great mass of the people are very poor and they live a hand-to-mouth existence upon a scale which Westerners would consider impossible. Day laborers, when they can get work, receive per day an amount equivalent to from ten to fourteen cents of our money, and upon this support their families. Money goes further there, however, the unit of their coinage being the "five cash" piece, a round brass coin with a hole in the center, worth about one tenth of an American cent.

But if the Koreans have their troubles, they also have their pleasures. They are great lovers of nature, and live out of doors much of the year. The men are fond of picnics. Several scholars will go to some picturesque spot and there compose spring poetry in Chinese. Or a party will spend hours in the practice of archery, at which they are quite skillful. If you happen to be in the country upon the occasion of a spring or fall holiday, you will hear the rhythmical clang of a brass gong, the staccato note of a tambourine beaten with a stick, or possibly the shrill tones of a brass clarionet.   Drawing near you will see a circle of young men and half-grown boys dancing, some of whom, perhaps, are dressed in female attire.   At a certain time each spring the Koreans indulge in stone fights, a rather rough kind of sport.   Two sides face each other with leaders wearing padded hats and carrying clubs.   These skirmish awhile with an occasional interchange of blows, and then the two sides rain stones at each other, much like a snow-ball fight.   Presently, with a mighty roar, one side begins to drive the other back.   Spectators catch the enthusiasm and join the attacking force.   The fun waxes fast and furious—so furious that not infrequently some one is maimed or killed.   Nothing that I have seen in Korea has given me such an impression of the latent force and fire in the usually apathetic Korean as this somewhat brutal sport.

Magistracies often keep a native orchestra. "Keesangs," or dancing girls, handsome, educated, dissolute, whose art consists largely in posturing, enliven the feasts of the official class.   Old men while away the time playing a native game resembling chess.   It must sadly be admitted that Koreans have their vices.   Lying is universal. Generations of practice have given them a wonderful skill in the art.   Business men continually cheat and overreach in their business transactions. A friend of mine, now a worthy Christian, told me that formerly his thought every morning as he awoke used to be, How can I cheat someone today? and that attitude of mind, I am led to believe, is common to a large class of Koreans. In spite of heavy penalties, stealing is frightfully common. Professional thieves carry great knives, and are handy in their use. Gambling, in spite of severe punitive laws, is widely practiced. Our harmless dominoes in Korea are used only for gaming purposes. Cards are also used that are long strips of cardboard the width of one's finger, bearing Chinese characters. Men become so frenzied with the gaming passion that, after losing everything else, they are known to stake and even lose their wives into slavery. The drink curse is widely prevalent in Korea. The liquors are of two kinds; one white and thick, the other a clear liquid. They are made from rice, barley or wheat. Saloons are frequent, with sauerkraut and liquor for sale. Maudlin sots or drunken brawls, with men tugging at each other's top-knots are, alas! a common sight upon the streets. Their thought is low-planed. The social vice prevails, and vice that is unspeakable. In a word, the Koreans have every vice possible to a mild-mannered, heathen nation, with the one exception of the smoking of opium. Let us turn to a subject more pleasing—the woman of Korea. She is frequently good-looking. She parts her glossy hair in the middle and combs it straight back, arranging it in a coil behind, at the base of the head, through which she thrusts an ornamental rod some six inches long, frequently made of silver. Her clothes are much like the men's, with trousers, padded stockings and sandals; but the jacket is very short, and she wears in addition an overskirt, high-waisted and reaching to within a few inches of the ground. A jaunty little cap with broad ribbons hanging behind is sometimes worn. In probably no respect does the life in heathen countries and in the lands that have felt the uplift of Gospel truth show so marked a contrast as in the position that is given to their women. In Korea, except where the influence of the missionaries has been felt, no man thinks of educating his daughters. Nearly every village has a Chinese school for boys; but not one for girls. With the exception of a very few rare instances, such as the lamented queen, no women outside of the keesang class have received a mental training. Here and there a woman can read Unmun. "Custom," hoary with age, that arch-enemy of all originality and progress, in Korea as in other parts of the Orient, fetters the people even to the minutest details of their life; and custom requires that the Korean women lead a life of great seclusion. From the time that the child first buds into the maiden until her face wears the tracery of old age, the respectable Korean woman is largely a prisoner within the four walls of the court of the women's quarters.   Let it be noted that the women in country villages, middle-aged women of the lower class, and Christian women in their attendance upon church meetings allow themselves greater freedom of movement. Occasionally on the streets may be seen a woman's closed sedan chair, with dangling, fan-like little red ornaments, and with a couple of coolies striding between the chair poles.   Or again a few women will be seen with long green cloaks or white skirts drawn over their heads so closely that of their features only a shining black eye is visible. But these occasional visits to the houses of relatives or friends are generally paid at night. In what a narrow world do they pass their lives! And then the women are universally spirit-worshipers, and live in constant dread of evil spirits.   In view of these facts, can we wonder that the habitual thinking of Korean women is petty, or superstitious, or vulgar?   Poor things!

It is easy to see, then, what a mental, moral and spiritual uplift the Gospel message brings to the women of the country.

The girl is married when a mere child, between the ages of twelve and sixteen, to a youth she has never known, and, as is the case in China, comes under the sway of her mother-in-law. If her mother-in-law is kind and her husband is good to her, a fair measure of home happiness awaits her. But the customs of the country all favor the married man rather than the married woman. He may divorce her upon any one of seven grounds—such, for instance, as inability to live at peace with her mother-in-law, or the absence of little ones from the home circle, especially the boys so necessary for the continuance of the ancestral worship. Then again, Confucianism throws its semi-religious sanction over the practice of the men's taking secondary wives or concubines. Large numbers of men in the middle and upper classes therefore take one or more concubines, whom they keep either in the same house, or in a separate building not far away, or in another village. As the man has some choice in these secondary attachments, it is very apt to be the case that the poor first wife has the respectability and the concubine has the love. Once again, marriage customs bear heavily upon the women, in that it is not considered respectable for a widow to marry again; although it is to be admitted that many a young widow, rather than face the burdens of life, becomes a concubine.

In the country, women are allowed much social freedom. I always like to watch a company of them hulling rice. The machine consists of a piece of timber shaped like a two-tined fork, and is hung on a pivot, with a cross-piece on the handle end that forms a hammer to pound the rice. One woman feeds the hole, where the hammer strikes, with unhulled rice. Then the bevy of women take hold of the straw ropes hanging

in the shed; they step upon the two prongs and
the hammer end rises; they step off and the hammer falls. Step on, step off. Chatter and laugh-
ter make the air melodious. Let us further consider the pursuits of the women. Korean house-
wives are accomplished needle-women. The
mode of washing and ironing clothes is peculiar.
Before washing, the seams are ripped and the
clothes are taken to pieces. Then beside the well,
or the brook outside the city, women of the lower
classes or the servants of the rich beat the clothes
into whiteness with flat wooden paddles. Ironing is done in the inner quarters of the house,
frequently into the small hours of the night. The
ironing is done with a large wooden roller that
may or may not be laid on a smooth block of
stone. Two or four ironing-sticks, like policemen's clubs, are used, depending upon whether
one or two women do the ironing. The pieces
of cloth are laid about the roller and, with a rhythmical tapping not unpleasant to hear, the clothes
are beaten stiff and smooth. Each autumn the
thrifty housewife puts down great jars of "sauerkraut" and pickled turnip for the winter use of
the family.

Little children in Korea certainly lead a happy
life; for whatever their other faults Korean men
and women love their little children and are kind
to them. These little ones ride astride of the
backs of father, or mother, or the six-year-old
brother or sister. In summer they toddle about,

as someone has remarked, "dressed in nothing
but a hair ribbon," or at most a short, quilted
jacket. When the New Year's season arrives, in
February, their fond mothers deck them out with
every kind of gayly-colored clothes. Would that
they might always remain so innocent and happy!

The small boy in Korea is much like the small
boy everywhere; his business in life is to play.
He makes a small hoop with a handle and fills
it full with a mass of cobwebs. Then with it he
catches insects. Or again, you will see him with
the end of a string tied about some large insect
which he allows to fly to the end of its tether.
In one or two instances I have seen him with a
centipede on the end of a string. I am sorry to
say he sometimes gambles, pitching "cash" at a
mark. At the New Year's season the sky is
bright with his tailless kites, made square with a
hole in the middle. The string is wound on a
four-armed reel that has something of the shape
of the reel of a binder, only it has a long
handle on one side fastened into the hub. The
boy, grasping the handle with one hand and a
corner of one of the arms with the other, twirls
this reel backward and forward very skillfully
and makes his kite go about the heavens in any
way he pleases. With these kites they fight,
crossing strings in the effort to saw each other's
string in two. And the custom is that the kite
that floats helplessly away anyone may keep
who can catch the severed string. Girls are fond

of playing at see-saw. A bag full of sand perhaps
a foot high is set on the ground. Across this is
laid a plank. Stretched alongside, at a proper
height for the children to grasp and steady themselves, is a rope. Two girls stand erect upon the
ends. One gives an upward spring and, as she
alights on the board, gives the other an upward
toss, who, as she alights in turn, throws the first
girl aloft a little higher. And so the sport goes
on, until in their upward flight each girl is thrown
two or three feet into the air. Frequent rests
are necessary, but the sport is the occasion of
much glee. In the springtime swings are set up,
which boys and girls alike enjoy. But the children must work as well as play. Many of the boys
go to school to learn to read and write Chinese.
Other boys in the country must trim branches
from the pine shrubs or rake the grass on the hill
sides to bind into great bundles of fuel, or scare
the armies of English sparrows away from the
yellow rice fields; while the girls must learn to
cook and do fine needle-work. Although Korean
children show great outward respect to their parents and to elderly people, I do not think that they
are trained to obey very well. Respectful greetings upon the part of children to older people are,
in the case of the boy, a complete prostration with
the hands on the ground and the forehead resting on the hands; the girl sinks downward in a
courtesy till her finger tips touch the floor; she
then steadily rises, folds her left hand beneath

her right arm and slowly sinks down as before. All boys and bachelors wear their hair in a braid down the back. When the latter marries he is allowed to put up his hair and wear a hat. I have been amused when sitting in a sarang with a group of men to see a slip of a boy with his hair done up in a top-knot enter, and note how respectful they were; a moment later a fine, sturdy young man, perhaps twenty-five years of age, with a braid down his back, appeared, and they all used low talk to him. The one was married, and the other was not. Korean men have three names, a boy name, often an opprobrious term, like "pig," so that the spirits may not become jealous of the honor shown him. The second and third are men's names, given when his hair is put up at the time of his marriage; one by which he is to be known familiarly among his friends, the other his formal, legal name. Girls have pretty names, meaning plum-blossom, treasure, etc. After their marriage they are known only as so-and-so's wife or the mother of so-and-so.

Just a word now about some of the characteristics of the Koreans. They are by nature rather a kindly people, and they treat us foreigners on the whole with much respect. It shows itself in such ways as this: A foreigner enters one of the tortuous lanes in which Seoul abounds, and which happens to be closed. Immediately a man or a small boy steps forward, politely explains that you cannot go that way and promptly points

out to you the proper road, and that, too, with no
apparent thought of remuneration.   With all their
many and glaring faults, one readily learns to love
the Koreans.   They are a hospitable people and
can be exceedingly polite.   Their politeness, too,
has a certain manly tone about it that one likes.
They are a leisure-loving people, full of curiosity and fond of sight-seeing.   Men will sometimes leave their families and be gone from home
for months wandering about the country.   Time
is no object to them.   Their actual knowledge
of the world they live in being small, and newspapers, until the last few years, being non-exist-
ent, their minds have been immensely interested
with very petty things.   For instance, men sitting
by the roadside can tell every mark on a horse
that has recently passed by.   News has a wonderful
way of traveling from mouth to mouth.   Let a
foreigner go down into the country to a certain
place and by nightfall every village within a radius of twenty miles is discussing him and all the
particulars connected with his arrival.   It is interesting to watch two Koreans engaged in a dis-
pute, for instance, over a business transaction.
Their voices are high pitched; they gesticulate
violently; they fairly rage at each other.   One
unaccustomed to their ways expects an immediate
casualty of at least a broken skull.   But as Mr.
Gale remarks, only a few minutes elapse before
they are seated at each end of a piazza quietly
smoking their pipes.   I have noticed something

similar in the scoldings fathers give their sons. The tones of the reproof were fairly blood-curdling. A moment later and the furious parent was as placid as a moonlit lake. A Korean gentleman rarely scolds other men; he lets his servant do it for him. This suggests another trait. Koreans, especially of the upper clases, have a distaste for unpleasant things; and if they have a hard thing to do or say they invariably get a third party to do it for them, wherever it is possible. Koreans who have learned to read a book or two in Chinese are apt to be inordinately conceited. As in China, a selfish individualism is only too characteristic of the great mass of the people. No man receives credit for being disinterested in anything he does. Patriotism and public spirit are practically undeveloped qualities in the minds of the Koreans. In political life there is incessant intrigue on the part of those out of office to displace by fair means or foul the holders of government position; and once in office their principal thought is that of the boa-constrictor—the desire to "squeeze" the people. Let it be noted, however, that there is now a small progressive party in Korea that finds its inspiration largely in a number of young men who have either held official position or studied for a number of years in the United States. Their mouth-piece is the *Independent*, a tri-weekly newspaper published in the vernacular by Phillip Jaisohn, M.D., an able young Korean nobleman, medically educated in the

United States, who has held a position in one
of the departments in Washington as an expert in
microscopy, is a member of a Presbyterian church
in Washington, is a naturalized American citizen,
and is married to an American wife. At present,
in addition to publishing two newspapers, one in
Korean and one in English, he holds the position
of adviser to the Department of Agriculture and
Commerce.

One who knows the Korean people, in spite
of all that has been or can be said of their
faults and vices, and of their listless apathy, so
largely the result of the conditions under which
they live, cannot help feeling that they have in
them the capacity for a high development when
once the truths of the Gospel have permeated the
mass of the people and when they can live in
security of life and property, under wise laws
righteously administered.

CHAPTER IV

A WEDDING IN KOREA

Among most peoples the wedding forms one of the most notable events in social life, and the Koreans are no exception to the rule. One bright morning in March, several years ago, we were informed that an opportunity was afforded us to witness a wedding conducted according to the Korean custom. The invitation was promptly accepted.

In company with two friends I took my way to a Korean hut near the wall, where a youth and his betrothed were about to make their bows to each other. Just as we arrived, the good-natured, round-faced fellow was donning his outer robes in an open space in front of the house.

According to Korean custom, he wore a costume like that which officials wear in royal audiences—one which he had hired for the occasion. The robe was a dark green, and bore "placques" with a pair of embroidered storks on the breast and back. About the wearer, like a hoop, was the black enameled belt, and on his head was a "palace-going" hat with wings on its sides, and finally he got himself into shoes that looked like "arctic" overshoes, two or three sizes too large for him.

At last he was ready to go indoors. An attendant preceded him with a red, flat-brimmed hat on his head, about his neck a string of beads, and in his arms a goose. The goose's feet were tied, and fastened through her beak was a little skein of red silk. In the two marched—three perhaps I ought to say. The court of the house had an awning of gunny-sacking suspended over it. Here a red table stood, with two red ornaments on it which looked like tall candlesticks, or sealed vases. The court was full of Korean men, women and children.

In front of the table the bridegroom bowed two or three times in the performance of a religious ceremony. And singular bowing it was. He gently lowered himself upon his knees, and then bringing forward his hands upon the mat, he bowed till his head touched the back of his hands. Then gracefully he resumed the standing posture. The last time he bowed he sank with the goose in his arms. I am told that the goose is the symbol of fidelity in Korea, it being popularly believed that if a wild goose dies its spouse never mates again.

By special invitation we then assumed a position upon the porch of the little house, facing the court. A mat was placed upon the steps, connecting with another mat on the porch. Presently the groom came to the front of the steps and stood there, while our attention was called to the room opening upon the porch. This room was filled with women, mostly young and more or less good-looking. I had caught a peep at the bride as she sat on a cushion.

But now she was coming out. Two middle-aged women accompanied her, each holding one of the bride's arms and guiding her steps, for her eyes were sealed completely. Clear up to her jetty hair, the face of the *petite* bride was painted a ghastly white. In the middle of her forehead and of each cheek were painted great, round, red spots; her lips were also bright red.

Her dress consisted of a bright green waist over a brilliant red skirt. Fastened through the coil of hair on the back of her smoothly combed head was a hair-pin, consisting of an ornamental rod, perhaps fifteen inches long. I remember it, for I almost got caught on it, in brushing by her later on.

Upon her head was a crown-like cushion, surmounted by half a dozen nodding sticks of beads, possibly three inches long. Down her back hung two broad brown ribbons, caught together with two ornaments, one a smooth, rectangular red stone, and the other a rosette of white jade, a stone precious in the East.

This little, painted, gorgeous creature was guided out, as I have said, by two middle-aged women. Across the mat they went, and at the end of the porch they turned the little bride about, and laid over her clasped hands a white handkerchief.

KOREAN YOUNG WOMEN.

The groom now stepped to the other end of the mat and the principal part of the wedding ceremony began. The bride made her bows. The attendants raised her arms till the small, draped hands lay level with the sightless eyes. Then, partially supported by the matronly women, she sank in a courtesy so profound that at the lowest point she was almost in a sitting posture. Then in the same slow, solemn manner she rose again. Her face at this time, and indeed during all the ceremony, was as expressionless as the face of a sphinx.

Three times this profound courtesy was repeated. Then it was the groom's turn. His face had more feeling in it than hers. Indeed, it looked flushed and anxious; much as a European's face might have appeared under corresponding circumstances. Our Korean groom now responded to his bride's greetings with two and a half bows, in which his head almost touched the floor. Then the bride and the groom were made to sit down upon their respective ends of the mat.

A table stood against the wall laden with what Koreans consider delicacies, but what they seemed to our perverted foreign taste I will refrain from stating, out of politeness to our host. Bread looking like a white grindstone, dishes of white, stringy vermicelli, bowls of "kimche," a native sauerkraut, candies, and a bottle of native liquor were there.

The couple were now sitting. The woman

nearest the table took a cup and filled it with liquor. This she touched to the bride's draped hands, and presented it to the groom. He took a sip, and handed it back. She refilled the cup, and they repeated the ceremony to the third time.

Then came a curious performance. The "go-between" had a part to do. She was the old lady with gray hair who had literally "made the match." She had attended to all the necessary preliminaries, even to doing the courting for the young people. The goose again appeared upon the scene. This time the skein of red silk had been removed from the holes in her beak.

Another woman held the bird, while the aged match-maker filled her hand with soft, stringy vermicelli, and offered it to her gray birdship. The goose eagerly dabbed away with her beak until she was nearly satisfied, when the old lady finished the ceremony by eating herself what was left in her hand.

All this had been done in the doorway leading into the bridal chamber. This room was now cleared of its young and middle-aged ladies, who were compelled to join the crowd in the court. To the bridal chamber the groom repaired and, removing his wedding robes, which made him look like an official, assumed garments more befitting his rank. His new costume consisted of a new white robe, and one of the ordinary broad-brimmed, conical-crowned hats.

He then came out, and the bride retired to the

room, to resume again her cushion on the floor; but just before she subsided into her placid meditations, her two attendants required her to bow to her foreign guests, and three times, without the movement of a muscle in her face, she sank to the floor in profound courtesies. We did not know just what was required of us at this juncture, but one after another, with perplexity written on our faces, we saluted the bride with American bows.

They were just arranging boxes with the view to feasting us with Korean delicacies, when the lady of our party reached the conclusion that it was time to retire. The motion was carried without debate, and amid many hospitable protests we made our farewells in our best available Korean phrases and withdrew, wishing for our hosts every possible blessing.

CHAPTER V

GUILDS AND OTHER ASSOCIATIONS *

If you were to stroll down the street leading from the West Gate to the center of the city of Seoul, and with observant eye should note the contents of the shops placed here and there along the way, you would notice at first a number of general shops. And in these booths, wide open to the street, you would see an assortment of goods probably something like this: a few articles of food, fine-cut tobacco, matches, hair ornaments, bright-colored pockets that look like tobacco pouches, and a few story books. It is noticeable that in these cluttered displays only a limited range of goods is to be seen. Further down the street, as you near the tower of the great city bell, the shops grow more substantial, and to see the goods of many of them you must go inside. In these

---

* This chapter is a picture of business conditions before the late war. During the "reform era," instituted by the Japanese, the office of magistrate of the market was abolished, the pu-sang office ceased to be numbered among the departments of the government, and the power of the merchants' and peddlers' guilds was broken. But since the conservative reaction set in, it is understood that the guilds have regained much of their ancient standing and power.

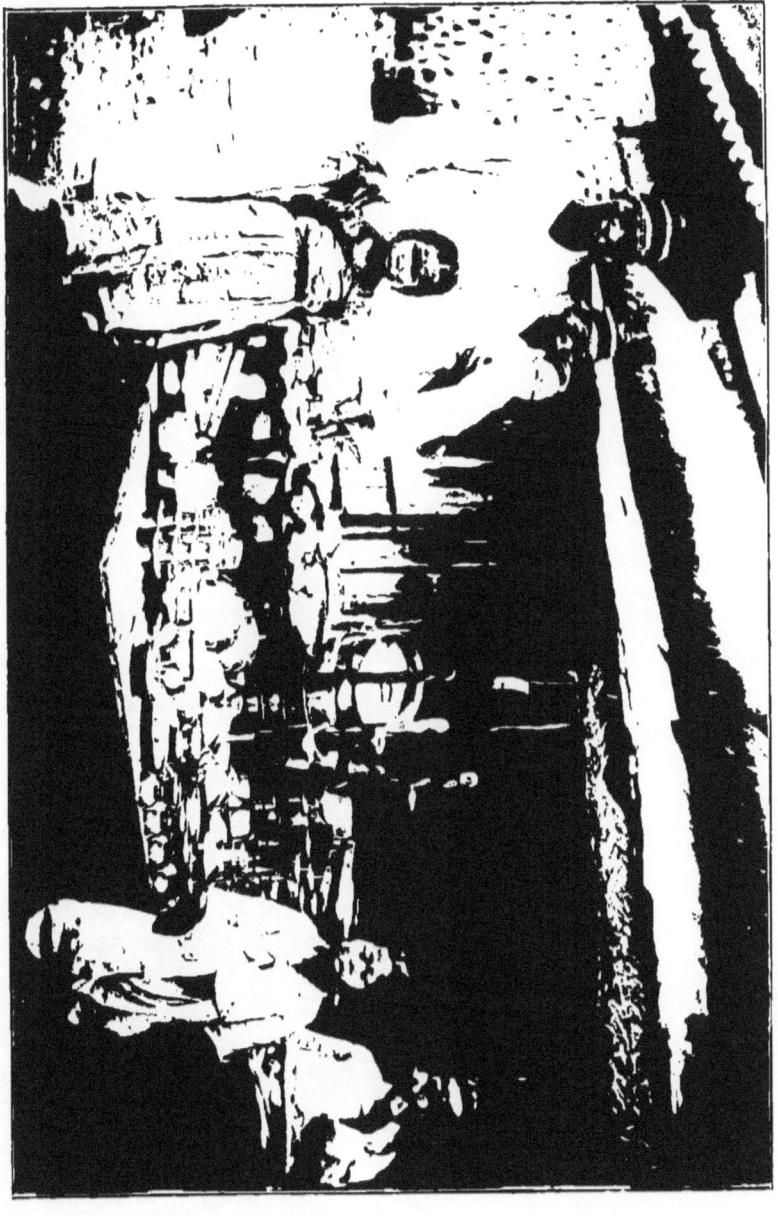

A Display of Brass Ware.

shops a merchant sells only one kind of goods, as paper, or shoes, or silk. But in the same shop several different shop-keepers may have their stalls. These men are the members of the merchant guilds. Any Korean can open a little general store. But certain lines of goods can be handled only by the members of trade guilds.

There are many different guilds corresponding to the different kinds of goods sold. For instance, the sandal trade, as distinguished from the trade in straw or string-shoes, is entirely in the hands of the shoe guild. One thing which seems curious to our Western notions is that the different kinds of cloth goods are handled each by a separate guild. There are guilds for cotton goods, for colored goods, for grass cloth, the gauzy summer goods, plain silks and figured silks. Then there are guilds for cotton, dyes, paper, hats, head-bands, rice, crockery, cabinets, iron utensils and brass ware. These are some of the principal trades of which the guilds have a monopoly. These guilds not only regulate their trade, but are mutually helpful in certain emergencies. For example, in case one of their number dies, they give financial aid to his family. Each guild has a head; and he with his servants is to be constantly found for the transaction of business at the guild headquarters. Should a man desire to enter into business in one of these monopolized trades, he must make application to the head of the guild. Should he prove acceptable, he must pay an entrance fee to the guild of, say $20. The head of the guild then furnishes him with a certificate of membership, duly made out and stamped with the seal of the guild, and the guild members come around and offer him their congratulations. He can then rent his stall or room and open up his wares whenever he likes. But suppose a man, without asking leave of the guild, should undertake to open a shop for the sale of silk or rice, what would happen? All would go well for a time; then one day his guild certificate would be called for. None being produced, a tempestuous time would ensue, the probable end of which would be that the guild would confiscate the contents of the shop. At all events, in a day or two there would be one less merchant in the silk trade. However, in this connection, a curious custom should be mentioned. From the twenty-fifth day of the last month of the Korean year, that is, during the last five days of the old year, and through the first five days of the new, Korean custom allows any one whatever to sell any kind of goods he pleases. Why it should be so I cannot tell, only such is the time-honored custom. This is the reason why the displays of shining brass ware are to be seen in all their glory upon the streets around Chong-No (the bell-tower place) at the New Year's season, while at any other time you must hunt for them among the shops, should you desire to see the handsome ware. While the guilds can cope successfully with intruders of their own people, they are powerless in the competition with the Chinese and Japanese merchants.

Members of guilds are required to pay a monthly tax to the head of their guild.

The government is accustomed to collect taxes from the guild, but applies directly to the head of the guild for payment. The patriotism of the guilds was shown upon the occasion of the burial of the dowager queen, when each guild added a large and beautiful silken banner to the gorgeous pageantry of the funeral.

Superior to either the guilds or their chiefs is an official appointed by the government to rule over the merchants. He may be termed the magistrate of the market. He holds the rank of *ban-sa*. At his government office he settles disputes between merchants, and acts as a judge in matters pertaining to commercial law. Not unlike the merchant guilds are the artisan guilds; what we would call at home "trades unions." But they are spoken of by a different name; for instance, the carpenters' guild or union would be known as the "room of the carpenters." Trades unions exist of the carpenters, the masons, the tilers, the chair-coolies, the rice-coolies, etc.

We come now to a form of guild, which, on account of its peculiar features, is deserving of a separate treatment. This is the peddlers' guild, known as the *pu-sang* guild. These need to be distinguished from the *po-sangs*, who are also merchants, who travel from market to market in the

country, but who in their organization are simply
the ordinary guild adapted to the conditions for
selling goods in the country.   The *pu-sang*, or
peddlers' guild, which we are now to consider, is a
very large and powerful guild.   In the country
villages shops are rarely found, but the buying
and selling of merchandise is done upon special
market days.   The country has been districted
among conveniently placed market towns, in
groups of five each, so that once in five days each
of these towns has its market day.   And peddlers,
for the most part belonging to this peddlers' guild,
keep traveling around these five-day circuits, carrying their stock of goods, one upon his shoulders,
another on an ox, and still another on pony-back.
But the peculiarity in the *pu-sang* guild consists
in their connection with the government.   In a
truly feudal sense are their services at the dis-
posal of the government.   Not one office, but
the higher officials of any government office, feel
at liberty to call in these peddlers for special services.   Is detective work required, these roving
peddlers can be made use of.   Does the king
desire to visit the ancestral graves, in the many
preparations which the occasion requires, such
for instance as the making ready the city streets
and country roads, the peddlers' services are
employed.   Or in the country, is a special escort
required for the guest of the magistrate, the services of the *pu-sangs* are called into requisition.
Mr. Gilmore's "Korea from its Capital," narrates

how Lieutenant Foulk, when naval attache of the American legation, had once a pleasing experience, while traveling in the country, of the courtesies of the *pu-sangs*, acting for him in the capacity of a night escort.* Especially are they liable to military service should the government have need to call an army into the field in addition to the troops in the barracks. So that,

---

* The following is the account mentioned above, that was written by Lieutenant Foulk, describing his experience with the *pu-sangs*:

"It was nightfall when we started to return. The magistrate, who was an officer of the *pu-sang*, brought his seal into use, and called out thirty of the body to light us down the mountains. Where these men came from or how they were called I did not understand, for we were apparently in an uninhabited, wild, mountain district. They appeared quickly—great, rough mountain men, each wearing the *pu-sang* hat. We descended the worst ravine in a long, weird, winding procession, the mountains and our path weirdly illuminated by the pine torches of the *pu-sang* men, who uttered shrill, reverberating cries continually to indicate the road or one another's whereabouts. Suddenly we came upon a little pavilion in the darkest part of the gorge; here some two hundred more *pu-sang* men were assembled by a wild stream in the light of many bonfires and torches. On the call of the magistrate they had prepared a feast for us here at midnight in the mountains. Here the magistrate told me he had been asked by the late minister to the United States, Min Yong Ik, to suddenly call on the *pu-sang* men of the Song-do district for services, to show me the usefulness and fidelity of the body; and he had selected this place, the middle of the mountains, and time, the middle of the night. I need not say that the experience was wonderful and impressive."

although Korea has no "merchant marine," she may be said to have a merchant soldiery.

Another curious feature is that among the great departmental offices of the government, such as the foreign office, the home office, and the war office, there is a *pu-sang* office for whose headquarters a large house is provided in the center of the city. And further, one of the greatest nobles in the country is the president of this office. In other words, he is the head of the *pu-sang* guild. Then the *pu-sangs* are subdivided according to magistracies, having what we would term a county organization, and there is a chief who is the head of all the *pu-sangs* in a given magistracy. Men who are not peddlers frequently join the peddlers' guild. A former gateman of ours, and in our neighborhood a paperer and one of the coolies are said to belong to the peddlers' guild. The popularity of the guild is due chiefly to its size and power. Not that they have any direct authority, but they are clannish in helping one another. For example, a *pu-sang* desires to collect a debt, but his debtor declines to pay. Does he put his note in the hands of a collection agency as we would at home? No, he mentions the matter to a few of his peddler friends. In the evening he calls again in company with these friends. And as twenty stalwart peddlers begin to bare their brawny arms, the debtor comes to the conclusion that he believes he *can* raise the money after all. But they have more legitimate modes of helpfulness. Like other guilds, they help each other in the case of special emergencies, such as a death or wedding in the family. On two occasions, I have seen great gatherings of the *pu-sangs*. They had large tents erected, and I remember that some of their number wore white straw hats, with a couple of cotton balls in the band. These were said to be low men in the order.

These various guilds, as we have seen, have characteristics in which they differ, combined with features that are similar. One of the family traits is the custom of mutual help with money or goods upon specified occasions. There are also certain varieties of another Korean association, known as the *kyei* or *kay*. The *kay* is a prominent feature in Korean social life. There are many varieties of these associations, organized for all kinds of purposes, some good, some bad. There are associations of which the Koreans themselves disapprove theoretically, as being organized for gambling purposes—lotteries in other words. Again, there are perfectly legitimate *kays*, which are insurance companies, or mutual benefit associations, or money-loaning syndicates. There are several different kinds of lotteries. One variety is limited in the number of those who engage, and has but one prize. Another kind has a hundred chances; and still a third has a thousand chances. Then there is one which the Koreans say has been copied after the foreign lottery, where tickets are sold in unlimited numbers. This is probably true, for I have seen the tickets of the Manila Lottery exposed for sale in the Chinese stores, instructing them in the ways of Western civilization. It is to the credit of the Korean government that it frowns severely upon these lotteries, and suppresses them where-ever it is possible.

We come now to the mutual-aid societies, insurance companies and loan associations. There is a form of *kay* which, considering the customs that govern it, would appear to be legitimate. A certain number of men belong to it; and they have a fortnightly or monthly casting of the lot. When a man has drawn the prize, he cannot try again until every other member has had his turn in drawing the prize. But whether eligible or not for the drawing, he must keep up his regular periodical payments to the manager of the *kay*. In some such associations, I am told, the amount of the sum drawn goes up month by month till a certain limit is reached, when it drops again to the original amount. We were surprised one Sunday on going to church to see the house-boy of one of our missionary friends standing with a fantastic tissue paper head gear on his head, and a native lantern in his hand, in a group of similarly furnished men outside a house where a funeral was to be held. He had to. He belonged to an association whose members are pledged to carry lanterns at the funeral, and furnish some stipu-

lated article, as the grass-cloth with which to wrap
the remains when one of their number dies.
Then there is another association which pays the
entire expense of the funeral, when death invades
the home of one of its members. These insurance *kays* are known by a number of names. In
contrast with these, there is an association whose
members are assessed when there is a wedding in
the family, or a young son puts up his hair in a
top-knot, and assumes the garb of manhood.
There is still another variety which helps at both
weddings and funerals. These insurance and
mutual-aid associations are conducted on the
assessment plan.

Koreans also associate themselves together in
kays for the purpose of loaning money. There
is one variety composed of people who loan their
money and divide the interest at the New Year's
season in order to lighten the heavy burden of
expense which custom connects with that festival
season. Another heavy item of expense in Korean families is the preparation of their winter
supply of certain articles of food, made in the fall.
Among their other preparations many families
salt down a large quantity of shrimps at this
season of the year. Hence it comes about that
there is an association whose members each spend
their portion of the accrued interest on their united
loan in buying the winter supply of shrimps.

It is a matter of course that every Korean
scholar wants to attend the royal examinations

once in a while. But for the poor country scholar attending the *koaga** is expensive, for, added to the cost of the examination paper, ink, etc., is the item of hotel bills on the way. So these scholars form an association, loan their money, and in the course of time divide the accrued interest, and find themselves in a position to attend the examination in Seoul.

The Koreans are very fond of going out of the city upon picnics in the spring, when the azaleas and other flowers are in bloom. So, festive but impecunious people sometimes form an association, loan their money, and use the interest in going out upon such excursions when the flowers are in their glory. Men who are fond of archery have their *kays*. Four or five archers meet and contribute a small sum each to form a prize, which is then given to the man most skillful with his bow. Or two sets of archers meet for a friendly contest, and the rich men and poor men among them, according to their several abilities, contribute a purse, out of which they provide a feast and dancing-girls to entertain them. Money is loaned by the *kays* at what we would consider very high rates of interest. Yearly loans are sometimes made, but more often money is loaned on ten months' time. In these ten-months' loans, if a man's credit is very good, he can borrow perhaps at 20 per cent. More often the rate charged is 30, 40, or 50 per cent. Thus 1,000 cash in the

---

* These *Koagas* were abolished at the time of the war.

course of ten months brings in an interest amounting to 200 cash, or more. Often the return payments are made during the ten months at the rate of one-tenth of principal and interest each month. Certain kinds of *kays* have each a manager, who is expected upon the occasions when they meet, once or twice a month, to furnish the members with wine or a meal. I once saw such a meeting in the country, and witnessed the casting of lots, when their names, written on white nuts about the size of a hickory nut, were drawn one by one from a gourd receptacle.

We sometimes think that in the home-land we have organizations for almost everything under the sun. But I am not sure whether Korean life, with all its different associations, is not about as complex as ours. The business world is certainly organized to an extent we are not acquainted with in Western lands. True, there are trades unions in each alike, but in Korea nearly all the merchants in the land are bound together in their powerful guilds, that are practically trades unions in the mercantile world. And it is worthy of note that one feature characterizes all these associations, whether merchant guilds, trades unions, the semi-political peddlers' guilds, or the legitimate kind of *kays*, and that is the trait of mutual helpfulness in time of need.

CHAPTER VI

The religious beliefs of Korea show a blending of Confucianism, Buddhism, and Shamanism. The Confucian learning, as we know, forms the basis of the education of the country. Every magistracy throughout the land has somewhere in its town a temple dedicated to Confucius, where, twice a year, in the spring and in the fall, the magistrate, with his numerous writers, worships the spirit of the sage. The social fabric of the country is largely Confucian. Ancestral worship is Confucian. Again, the monasteries and temples of Buddha are scattered throughout the country— a faith with much of its lustre gone. Frequently before a village door may be seen a couple of monks or nuns soliciting alms, as they tap upon their wooden begging-bowls in time to a monotonous chant. Socially, they hold nearly the lowest position, and until the time of the war were forbidden to enter the gates of Seoul. Shamanism, or Spiritism, has its representatives in the blind sorcerer, the *mutang*, or sorceress, and the geomancer who chooses fortunate grave sites.

Each religion furnishes its share to the mythology of the country. At the head of their system of belief is Hananim, whom the Chinese

recognize as Shangti. Many would introduce as
next inferior to him Buddha (indeed, some go to
the temples upon the death of a relative to pray
the Buddha to send his spirit to the good abode).
Then come the ten judges of hades, whose pictures may be seen in Buddhist temples. Through
their servants they are said to be well versed in
the affairs of mortals. Upon the death of a man,
one of his souls is seized by official servants of
these judges and hurried to hades. The judges,
knowing whether his deeds have been good or
evil, give sentence, and in accordance with the
judgment the spirit is sent either to the Buddhist
heaven or to the Buddhist hell to spend the rest
of his existence. In the latter place are manifold
kinds of punishment. For you must know that,
while many Koreans believe with the Southern
Buddhists in the transmigration of souls, many
others follow the Northern cult in the belief in a
heaven and a hell. Another class of Koreans
believe that the soul does not go to the realm of
departed spirits, but wanders about on this earth
dependent for its condition upon the fidelity of
his sons in keeping up the prescribed sacrifice.
Next below the ten judges come the *sansin*, or
mountain spirits. Each mountain on the checker-
board of Korea is supposed to have its presiding
genius in the person of a mountain spirit, of
whom more anon. Below the mountain spirits
are many other kinds of spirits. We come now
to the *kuisin*, or devils. Nearly all the women

and three-fourths of the men of Korea stand in mortal terror of these malevolent beings. Is any one sick, or in trouble, going on a journey or moving his lodgings, the demons are propitiated by sorcery.

With this brief look at the religions of the country, let us center our attention upon the ancestral worship as practiced in Korea. Ancestral worship is Confucian in its origin. Confucius was intensely practical in his philosophy. His mind took no pleasure in dwelling upon the supernatural. He said: "Spirits are to be respected, but to be kept at a distance." On another occasion he said: "While you are not able to serve men, how can you serve their spirits?" He found ancestral worship existing among the ancients he so much venerated, and he passed on the custom almost without comment. And yet, while he set before men a beautiful array of virtues to be practiced, because he gave to the virtue of filial piety an excessive importance and made it the foundation stone of his structure, he may be said to have furnished the *principle* for ancestral worship.

The customs regulating ancestral worship in Korea are so interesting, that it may be profitable to consider the procedure after death somewhat in detail. Koreans believe that every man has three souls, and upon death one goes to hades, or wanders about on the earth, one goes to the grave, and one takes his abode in the ancestral tablet.

In the last moments before death, silence reigns through the house. Sad ministrations follow, and the remains are placed in new clothes for burial. Outside the door is at once placed a little table with three bowls of rice, and a red squash; and alongside of it are ranged three pairs of straw shoes.

Three official servants have come to take the soul to the ten judges in hades. These are presents to them. Smelling the flavor of the cooked rice, they are refreshed. The shoes being burnt, they are shod for the journey. The squash is a present to the prison official who lived 2,000 years ago, and was fond of squash. Then the rice is thrown away, and the squash broken. This is done during the first half-hour after death. Then the inner garments of the deceased are taken out by a servant, who waves them in the air and calls loudly to the deceased by name. At the same time the friends and relatives of the dead man loudly lament. After a time the clothes are thrown upon the roof of the house and left there.

The choice of the site of the grave is considered a matter of great importance to Koreans. The semi-globular mounds are invariably placed upon hillsides. While they may be placed upon slopes facing any direction, a south exposure is preferred, probably for reasons such as carry weight in China, the belief being there that inasmuch as warmth and life proceed from the south, and cold and frost from the north, that grave is most fortunately located which is at the same time sheltered from the north and open to the good influences supposed to emanate from the south. But if that were all, the choice of a grave site would be a simple matter. There are many intricate points connected with the subject, in which only the initiated are versed. The relatives are obliged to consult a geomancer. He is a learned man who, by long study of books upon the subject in his possession, knows all the superstitions relating to the good and bad influences supposed to be in the ground. He must choose the burial site. It is believed that a well-chosen site brings rank and money and numerous sons to the children of the one buried there.

The day of the funeral arrives. The remains have been placed in a coffin more or less expensive, according to the means of the family. At dusk they start with a long train of lanterns, the brilliantly colored hearse, the loudly weeping mourners, of whom the male members are dressed in the bushel-basket hat and the yellow mourner's clothes. The grave at last has been reached, the interment has taken place, and the mound has been rounded up. Now occurs the first sacrifice. Small tables are placed in front of the grave. Upon them are set offerings of wine and dried fish. The relatives, facing the offerings and the grave, bow to the ground in five prostrations. A formula is repeated, wishing peace to the spirit who is to dwell in the grave. Afterward, at a

little distance behind the grave, like offerings
and similar prostrations are made to the mountain spirit. The mountain spirit is supposed to
preside over the place. Prayer is offered to him,
invoking his protection as host to the spirit in the
grave they are committing to his care. This is
deemed necessary in order to secure hospitable
treatment for the spirit at the grave. After these
ceremonies the wine is disposed of, and the fish
is divided among the servants.

We now come to the third soul of the man.
He returns from the grave with the mourners
to take up his abode in the ancestral tablet. In
the room the tablet is to occupy (a vacant room
if possible) another offering is made.

The offerings consist of native bread, wine,
meat, cooked rice and vermicelli soup. These
articles of food are placed before the tablet that
the spirit may regale himself with the flavor.
The relatives and friends bow five times. Then
the food is taken into another room and eaten by
the assembled company.

At this point it may be well to make a few
explanations. The ancestral tablet consists of a
couple of strips of whitened wood, put face to
face, with a hollow space cut into their inner sur-
faces, and within which are written upon one of
the strips, in Chinese, the family name and other
writing. A small round hole connecting this
inner space with the outer air is supposed to give
ingress and egress to the spirit. The tablet thus

constituted is slipped into a socket in a wooden block, and thus adopts an upright position, following which it is placed in a protecting case. After three years of mourning it is put with the other ancestral tablets in the little cabinets in the ancestral temple adjoining the house. During the intervening time, if the man is wealthy he places the tablet in a vacant room, usually in his wife's apartment. But if the man is poor and has no ancestral temple, the tablet is placed in a box on one side of the room, and on the occasions when he worships his other ancestors, strips of paper with writing on them are pasted on the wall in lieu of the proper tablets. The common people worship not only for their father, but also for their grandfather and great-grandfather. Some go back two generations or more. High officials worship for four, while the king worships for five ancestors.

Some curious customs regulate the period of mourning, strictly so called.

If the father dies, the family goes into mourning for three years. If the father and mother die the same day, the same period of mourning is observed; and likewise, should the mother die some time after the father's death. But if while the father is alive the mother dies, the family wear mourning garments for one year.

Again, suppose three generations of a family to be living. The father dies, and the family goes into mourning for three years. The grandfather dies next, and the son takes his dead father's place in wearing mourning clothes for another three years. Where a man received rank, posthumous rank is sometimes given to his departed father from the feeling that the father must always be considered higher than the son. An official cannot hold office during the three years of mourning. And we remember how, in the year of mourning for the Dowager Queen, custom required that the public offices be closed for a long period of time. Custom also prescribes that no matter how young a king may be at the time of his decease, his successor must be younger than he, so that he can perform the sacrifices.

But to return to the family in mourning. Allusion has been made to the mourning clothes ordinarily worn. On the minor sacrificial occasions, a peculiar robe is worn. It consists of a flowing-sleeved garment, split up the back to the waist, over which division a fold falls to the bottom of the garment. During the three years, upon the two national mourning days, and upon the anniversary of the father's death, an especial attire is worn by the male relatives during the ceremonies of mourning. Among other features the official hoop belt is worn; and the hat is peculiar, in which a white loop goes up over a baggy skull-cap from front to rear.

During the three years a dish of fruit is constantly kept before the ancestral tablet.

Let us consider the sacrifices further demanded

by the laws of ancestral worship.   Upon all these occasions the eldest son is invariably the master of ceremonies.   During the three years certain sacrifice is rendered only before the deceased father's tablet, and not in the ancestral temple. On the first and fifteenth of each Korean month sacrifice is performed, and rice or vermicelli soup, amid lamentations, is placed before the tablet. The time for the sacrifice is one or two hours after midnight.   The anniversary of the father's death is a very important occasion during the mourning years.   While in mourning, on the night before this anniversary, sacrifice is made before the tablet.   The next morning friends visit the family in mourning, and sympathize with them, upon which occasion food in many varieties is set before them.   Some time during the day the mourners repair to the grave and repeat the sacrifices of the previous year to the soul in the grave and to the mountain spirit.

These constitute the sacrifices peculiar to the first three years.   Afterward the offerings upon the first and fifteenth days cease, while sacrifice on the father's anniversary day goes on perpetually, but in the ancestral temple where the other tablets are.   Mention should be made here of the anniversaries of the grandfather's and great-grandfather's death, when sacrifice is made in the ancestral temple, and at their graves.

We come now to the eight Korean holidays upon which sacrifice to the dead must be performed.

The occasions are New Year's day (about the 1st of February), the fifteenth day of the first month which closes the New Year's holiday season, the two national mourning days, and four other festivals. Upon these days sacrifice is offered at daybreak. One peculiarity marks the celebration of these eight festivals during the mourning years. A double sacrifice is performed at the house; one in the ancestral temple before the remoter ancestors' tablets, the other later, before the father's tablet in the other building. The two general mourning days come in the spring and in the fall; one in the third month, corresponding to April, the other in the eighth month, our September. Upon these two days the practice is various. Some visit their father's grave, and some do not. Others again visit in addition the graves of their grandfather and remoter ancestors, upon which occasions they bow and offer their food at the graves and before the presiding mountain spirit.

Now, as to the significance of all this ancestral worship. The literature upon the ancestral worship of China, especially the pamphlet by Dr. Yates, seems to indicate that the Chinese believe that the happiness of the dead and of the living is directly connected with ancestral worship. Whether their fathers are rich or beggars in the other world depends upon the fidelity of their children in keeping up the prescribed sacrifices, and they are believed to reward or punish the living children according to their faithfulness in ancestral worship.

Many Koreans would agree with this view. Still another class seem to believe that the condition of the dead is permanently fixed by the sentence of the ten judges upon their arrival in the other world. Such would hold that whether a man worships his father or not, does not affect the happiness of either the father or the son. But it does affect the reputation and social standing of the son among his acquaintances, as being a man who shows respect or disrespect to the spirit of his father living in the ancestral tablet in his house. Such are some of the features of the ancestral worship of Korea.

CHAPTER VII

As I was told at a monastery near by that I was the first foreigner who had visited this noted mountain, it may prove of interest if I relate my experiences while there. As to the question of where it is, I would state in the province of Chung Chong, perhaps ten miles south of Kong-Ju, the capital, a little off from the main road that leads to the south. Kay-riong-san is a notable mountain, whether for itself or for its venerable monasteries, but more especially because it rises not far from the spot which, tradition tells us, is to be the site of the future Seoul of the next dynasty, whenever it comes. The natives put it thus: The founder of the present dynasty had determined to locate his capital there, and had been three days at work on the walls, when the mountain spirit warned him off. The site was not for him. He must locate at the present Seoul. The property was being held for the dynasty that would follow his own. And as his majesty had no desire to engender the ill-will of the local deities, he prudently withdrew his claim.

The mountain is magnificent; as high as Pyok-Han to the north of our city of Seoul. But instead of a cluster of glorious peaks, there is a suc-

99

cession of perhaps a dozen such peaks in picturesque irregularity. On the side of our approach they were green with splendid timber to
their very summits. I think that one gains a more
vivid sense of their majesty from the plain,
because the eye sweeps up over comparatively unbroken slopes of green to the tremendous peaks
above. I cannot soon forget the approach to the
monastery at the foot of the mountain. Splendid
trees centuries old lined the avenue, through whose
interstices came the sunlight and glimpses of the
majestic green mountains. Birds were singing,
while here and there could be heard the music of
cascades. We arrived at the monastery. Here
were buildings that were erected at the time when
our fathers wore armor or wolf-skins in the train
of Emperor Charlemagne, a thousand years ago.
One temple into which we looked, that was six
or eight hundred years old, impressed us as
having been built when Buddhism was in its glory.
The fine large statues of the three seated Buddhas
and of their attendants beside them, together with
the platform on which they were placed, towered
aloft some fifteen feet. The wooden frame which
held the drum of the monks consisted of two
very well-carved dragons. In another building was the finest bell I have seen in Korea.
Upon its sides were carved the names of the faithful who had given it. It hung from its frame by
a loop of well-made dragons of bronze. In one
of the thousand-year-old buildings time had been

unkind to the Buddha. Half of his dainty mustache was wanting, and the gold was gone from his fingers. In another building were four large pictures of noted priests. One with a flowing black beard represented Sa-Miong-Tong, who it is said went to Japan, in the days of the invasion, and by his magical arts intimidated the Japanese into concluding a peace with Korea. Such is the tradition. The persimmons growing at this monastery were the finest I tasted in Korea. We saw a foundry in which the monks make kettles, such as the natives use for the cooking of food. Standing by itself in a rather wild place rose a curious iron tower. Iron cylinders, perhaps two feet in diameter, were placed one upon another to the height of forty feet. Two tall stone slabs helped to support the tower. The last ten feet of the cylinders leaned away at an angle from the almost perpendicular shaft. The top of the column had an ornamental capital. I could get no satisfactory explanation of the shaft. In another spot we saw a small pagoda upon whose shelves sat a number of little stone Buddhas, some with heads and some without, but all of them serene in posture. I glanced into one of the monastery kitchens. Above one of the huge cooking-places, painted upon the wall in bright colors, was a kitchen god. He had the look of a large well-fed Korean seated in a chair with a couple of attendants beside him. After tiffin my Korean friend proposed that

while our horses went around, we follow the
path over the brow of the mountain.   A look
at the steep tremendous peak filled me with no
great enthusiasm. However we went.   A slender
young monk put on a yellow-peaked sun-bonnet
and led the way.   He had come but recently
from Seoul to take up the life of a monk, and the
poor fellow was evidently homesick. We had
been climbing some time when we came to
another monastery.   Its calm, gilded Buddha sat
in a glass case.   Here we had a change of guides.
He was a fat young monk, as merry as an early
spring robin.   Up we zigzagged over a rugged
path.   At the summit was another monastery in
whose court, strange to say, stood a Japanese
glass street lamp.   Here I saw an elderly monk,
the first really ascetic Korean monk that I have
met.   His head was shaven, his face looked thin
and worn, and his manners were charmingly
gentle.   After a rest we took in the splendid
view.   To the north and south were a profusion
of mountains.   Southward we looked over nine
successive peaks. Westward the country stretched
in a comparatively unbroken level to the sea.

A third bright young monk led us down the
mountain to the large monastery at its foot, where
we were to spend the night.   In the dim twilight
of the following morning we heard a tap-tap, tap-
tap, tap, tap, as the wooden part of the great
drum was struck.   Then came the loud sound of
the drum.   Next the boom of the great bronze

bell, which sounded now and again during the strange, monotonous chant of the monks that followed. It all seemed very weird to one's half-wakened senses. Later we visited the famous plain to which allusion has been made. Two monks, one in the small yellow begging-hat, shaped like a bowl, and the other in the ordinary wide-brimmed, round-crowned, black monk's hat, who had occasion to go in the same direction, showed us the way. Presently we found ourselves climbing the mountain, green with bushes and grass. We were entering by the western approach. Not far from the top of the ridge we saw a brook that slipped for fifty feet down a slope of rock at an angle of forty-five degrees. From here our path led down a valley which furnished one of the roughest pieces of road that I ever traveled. The brook that went with us was falling all the time, and it was with the greatest difficulty that we kept from following its example. One of our party did rest for a time in one of the puddles of the road. One of the many cascades of the valley deserves particular mention. To view it well required a visit in one's stocking feet. The wide brook dropped with a sheer fall of twenty-five feet into an oval pool that was green in color and of unknown depth. The natives say that in the depths of the pool sleeps a male dragon. Presently the rocky road opened upon a great plain. As we traveled through it we saw where the canal had been begun that was to have crossed the city. Soon we reached the place where huge cubes of stone lay about the plain in careless disorder. These the ancient king had cut and brought from the hills, when he thought to build his city here. Under almost every block of stone holes had been scraped. It is said that the natives at one time brought nails and placed them under the stones, in the belief that by so doing they would be rid of disease. But doubt having been raised as to the value of the remedy, the nails were all dug out and used. As we looked about, this place was pointed out as the spot where the palace was to have stood. And from yonder knoll the great bell was to have tolled its warning that day was done, and that the stream of life throbbing through the great gates must rest until the morrow.

But what a site for a city! An enormous level plain, amply sufficient to hold a great population, wonderfully fortified by the hand of God in the mountains that he built about it. To the north were grand, rugged, mountain heads. To the east and west more regular ridges. To the south the plain opened out upon a chorus of peaks of all heights and sizes. The east, north, and west approaches would probably have been difficult. But from the south the city would doubtless have been easy of access. Had the founder of the present dynasty placed his capital here, he could have made for himself an almost impregnable city;

but his choice of Seoul was undoubtedly wise, for he gained thereby a capital of far more central location.

CHAPTER VIII

THE FEAR OF DEMONS

The merit of the little poem,"Seein' things," by
that melodious singer of childhood's thoughts,
Eugene Field, consists not in the scientific accuracy of the boy's deductions, but in the fact that it
enables us to see the horrid phantoms of the night
through the eyes of the boy. In like manner,
please consider that this chapter is not an attempt
at a scientific investigation in the realm of demon-
ology, but simply an effort to let you view the
occult beings they so much dread from the point
of view of the average Korean.*

No one can understand the inner life of the great
majority of the Korean people who fails to take
note of their attitude toward these demons. When
the Korean thinks of these beings no warm surge
of love and joy comes into his heart, as is the case
with the Christian when he is filled with the
thought of his Father in Heaven, but rather his
imagination peoples the earth, the sea, the sky,
the haunts of men and the wilderness with
myriads of spirits, five-sixths of whom are hate-

---

*For most of my knowledge upon this subject I am
indebted to the researches of Rev. G. H. Jones, Mrs. Gifford
and the late Dr. E. B. Landis.

ful, wicked, malicious, and the other one-sixth, while better disposed, are capricious in the extreme. These beings have it in their power, he believes, to bring him material prosperity or to injure him and his family in a thousand different ways—such, for instance, as through the loss of property, or sickness, taking frequently the form known as "demon possession." He can never tell when he has offended one of these beings, so he, and more especially his wife, live in a constant dread that impels them to frequent expensive offerings to appease their jealous anger. Demon-worship takes no thought of the joys or woes of a future life, presents not one inducement to men to live more moral lives, but strikes incessantly upon the one emotional chord of fear. It has been estimated that demon-worship costs the people of Korea two million five hundred thousand dollars every year. In the city of Seoul alone three thousand sorceresses ply their art, earning, on an average, fifteen yen a month apiece—a very good living, indeed, according to Korean standards. Thus some idea can be formed of the hold this demon cult has upon the lives of the people. It is undoubtedly *the* religion of the country, as well as the oldest of all its beliefs.

To consider from the Korean point of view these supernatural beings more in detail, they are divided into two classes, each of which is again capable of a further subdivision. The first and larger class consists of malicious fiends and the spirits of men who have died in poverty, or under other painful circumstances, and now wander about the world in cold, hunger and nakedness, wreaking their spite on all who refuse to supply their needs through offerings. The second class embraces spirits of a kindlier nature and the shades of men who in this life were prosperous and influential. The people believe that by proper inducements in the form of offerings, incense and prayers, they can buy off members of the first class or prevail on others of the second class to interest themselves in their behalf. Go into the inner court of a Korean home and among other evidences of spirit worship you would probably see the following fetishes or spirit "nests": Somewhere out of doors in the court is visible a bundle of straw set on some sticks or a shelf containing a scrap of cloth or a bit of straw rope and upon which on the offering days, the 1st, 2d, 3d, and 15th of the month, cooked food is placed. This is the nest of the spirit of the site. Again, in the shed room used for a kitchen, the fetish of the kitchen demon may be seen in a piece of cloth or paper fastened to the wall above the fireplace. In the deep veranda attached to the side of the great beam overhead are seen paper and rice, representing the abode of the spirit of the ridgepole, who occupies rather a chief position among the household spirits, and who is supposed to bring to the home a measure of health and happiness, and yet is unable always to ward off sick-

ness.   At the approach of a contagious disease he
is said to flee from the premises and must be
coaxed back with proper ceremonies later on.
The rites attending the introduction or recall of
this spirit into a home have been thus described:
The house having been cleaned and a feast prepared, the *mutang*, or sorceress, who has been
called for the occasion, starts out to hunt the spirit.
She ties a good-sized sheet of paper around an
oak rod, which she holds upright in her hand.
She may find the spirit just outside the house or
she may have to go some distance before he indi-
cates his presence by shaking the rod with so
much force that many men with their united
strength could not hold it still.   He accompanies
the *mutang* as she returns to the house.   Upon
their arrival great demonstrations of joy are made
that he has come to bless the family with his presence.   The paper which was tied around the stick
is folded, soaked in wine, a few pieces of cash
slipped into it and then tossed against a beam in
the house, to which it adheres.   Rice is thrown
up, some of which sticks to the paper, and the
spirit nest is complete.   Smallpox creates great
ravages among the little folks of Korea, and parents never count their infants among the number
of their children until they have had that disease.
They believe there is a smallpox devil, to whom
the name of *Mama* has been given, and whose
home they say is in the south of China.   The
well-known symptoms break out upon a baby.

At once a *mutang* is called, and under her direction they proceed to do the spirit reverence. The parents bow low before the sick child and address it continually in terms of the highest respect. If the child survives, at the turn of the disease the *mutang* is called again, a feast is prepared and the smallpox devil is bidden adieu, with many polite wishes for a prosperous journey to his native land. This shows something of the inner life of Korean homes. Every day in the month is considered fortunate for the doing of certain things and unlucky for the doing of certain others, so fettered are they by their superstitions.

Strangers in Korea have their curiosity aroused by seeing here and there by the roadside a small tree growing apparently out of the midst of a pile of stones. To its limbs are attached all manner of white rags, shreds of colored cloth and pieces of paper, some of which contain written prayers. Coolies going by spit at the pile. Old women with little bundles of clothing tied to the tops of their heads and a staff in one hand, pause and bow reverently, rubbing together their palms. An evil spirit dwells in the tree and it is considered wise in travelers to show him some mark of attention, exhibited in these different ways. Food is sometimes offered at these stone piles to wandering hungry spirits. Here and there a great splendid tree is considered haunted. Sometimes upon the crown of a mountain pass you will come upon a spirit shrine. Within you will see colored pictures. One is of an old man sitting on a tiger; handsome women, apparently his wives, stand about, and beyond are the pictures of retainers. This is the shrine of a mountain spirit. The people will point out to you pools, where great writhing dragons are said to have their homes. Near many a country village may be seen a rude shrine where some great local spirit is worshiped every three years, and the expenses of the festival are defrayed by public taxation.

The priests and priestesses of this "unorganized Shamanism" are blind men called *pansus* and the women termed *mutangs*. If you could only forget the horrid meaning of it all, the dancing of the *mutang* in her worship, in time to the beat of the gong and the drum in the shape of an hour-glass, would impress one as quite picturesque. She is supposed to be under the control of a spirit of influence in the realm of darkness, who, for a consideration, can be induced to appease the injured dignity of some malignant spirit who is afflicting a household. She also claims the power to foretell future events. No matter what her position in life, the call of a woman by a spirit to become a *mutang* is considered irresistible. She will make plenty of money, but at a high price; for she becomes a social outcast, not on moral grounds, but by reason of her vocation. The *pansu* deals directly with the evil spirits, which he drives away by repeating exorcisms from a book handed down from the earliest ages, whose

words are meaningless at the present time. One
of his many pretensions is the bottling of a foul
spirit. Under ordinary circumstances it is only
necessary to offer some poor food, meanly prepared and offered in coarse dishes, with an order
to cease their persecutions, which may be in the
form of sickness or mysterious manifestations, such
as unaccountable noises, unexplained fires in roofs,
the mysterious finding of sieves and articles of
clothing in the tops of trees. If this proves
insufficient, the fiend is called and is supposed to
manifest his presence by causing the small bit of
wood which has been placed on the floor in front
of the *pansu*, to dance in a most extraordinary
manner. The *pansu* chastises him severely with a
stick which he grasps in one hand, and drives him
into a wide-mouthed, empty bottle which he holds
in the other. When this is accomplished, which
is indicated by the piece of wood hopping in, the
bottle is corked, buried at a cross-roads and a fire
is built over the spot. These are some of the
methods employed by the *pansus* and *mutangs*.

Let us consider the attitude of the Korean
Christians, more especially toward' what they
regard as cases of demoniacal possession. The
following is the naïve account given by a Korean
Christian man living on the island of Kang-wha
to Mrs. G. H. Jones, which she inserted in one of
her annual reports to the Northern M. E. Mission.
He was an eye-witness of the events he narrates:

"There was a man living in Sosa Sirimi on

A Wayside Idol.

Kang-wha, who has since removed to Chemulpo.
With his entire household he became a Christian,
and although he had not as yet received baptism,
he cast away all his idols and ceased from the
evil deeds of the past.   On the eve of the ninth
day of the sixth moon his wife, though sick, had
no pain, yet her limbs became rigid like a dead
person and she was totally unconscious.   Being
thus the whole night, we thought she had the
Asiatic cholera, and gave her medicine.   When
daylight came she seemed to be better and we
concluded she had recovered.   The next night
she had a return of the attack, going into convul-
sions and becoming unconscious.   Three or four
persons were called in to rub her limbs and we
gave her medicine again and again.   At daybreak
she recovered.   This time we believed she was
entirely cured; but at about six o'clock in the
evening the attack returned.   Her husband rubbed
her limbs.   Three or four of the brethren were
present.   In an hour she awoke and began to
gnaw her hands, so that her mouth was bloody.
Those standing by, using in fun the words
employed to drive out a dog, cried 'Egai! Egai!'
and she began to bellow.   Therefore all were
astonished and cried, "This is not cholera.   A
devil has taken possession of her.   We must
beseech the Lord to cast it out.   Let us pray.'
Then the sick woman, with evident grief, began
to cry again.   We inquired why she cried.   She
answered: 'You call me a devil; and say you will

drive me away.' Therefore we were sure it was the devil. This being Friday evening and the time when the women meet for prayer, all of the sisters and some of the brethren met at the sick woman's house, and reading Mark 5:1-20, with one heart all besought the Lord, saying: 'Lord have pity on us. We are all sinners, and very weak, and when the devil tries us, we are defenseless. Oh, Lord, bring to pass what we have just read in the Bible. Make the devil to leave this woman and go to his own place.' As we prayed the woman sat up and joined in our prayer. And then when we sang, she sang with us. We all exhorted her to have faith that the devil had been cast out, and give no place to doubt; to beseech the Lord to never again allow the devil to disturb her. Then, praising God, we all dispersed to our homes. From that time she was entirely cured and to this day she is a whole person. Thus the Lord favors us; but how many are ignorant of his grace. The spirit of which she was possessed is called *Sai-pyol-sang*, and is very wicked. If one should serve it, it will be difficult to eat food brought in from another house, and if the attempt is made to eat without first having prayed to the spirit, sickness will result. It is also difficult to bring into the house clothing. If a person brings a bright-colored cloth into the house without first acknowledging the spirit, sickness will surely result. This family having once worshiped the spirit and now propos-

ing to cast it away, received this trial; for on the
day the woman took sick, some new cloth had
been brought into the house, and the devil being
angered at thus being ignored punished his former
slaves." Thus closed his narrative. Mrs. Jones
says that she supposes the physicians would pro-
nounce it a case of hysteria; but whatever this
may have been, the Christians feel that she was
healed by their prayers.

Certain it is that for many a Korean the abandonment of spirit-worship is one of the most
serious steps than can possibly be taken. Here
is an instance in point. A female inquirer who
felt it her duty to give up the worship, and doubt-
ing her own courage, called in Miss Ellen Strong
of our mission to help her destroy the implements of worship. At the appointed time she
came and found the woman looking deathly pale
and fairly sick from a sense of the seriousness of
the step she was about to take, and rather disposed to give up the effort. It took considerable
persuasion upon the part of Miss Strong to get
up her courage to the point of action, and then
she had to take the initiative in the destruction of
the spirit "nests" and the other utensils. Only
when the operations were well under way did her
hostess venture to take an active part in the pro-
ceedings. We are utterly unable to appreciate the
terror which, under such circumstances, must fill
the heart of a Korean woman who had lived
all her life under the fear of the demons.

The following extract from a report of Mrs. J.
S. Gale, made to one of the annual meetings of
our mission, admirably shows the change that
comes into the lives of Koreans when they pass
from demon-worshipers to followers of Jesus
Christ: "In the early spring" (1895) "Mrs. Kim
and Mrs. Kwon came to me, and they said their
husbands had been attending the men's meetings
upon the hill, and they had heard that Jesus
Christ could cast out devils, and that was just
what they wanted him to do for them. Their
houses were full of evil spirits, they said. They
could not sleep for the strange sights and sounds.
Sometimes it seemed as if sand were dashed
against their windows, and again as if water were
being poured from one dish into another. Night
after night they had searched for the cause of
these disturbances, with no other result than to
find the cup-boards and dishes moving about the
house in a mysterious way, and large earthen
jars placed inside others which had such narrow
necks that none but supernatural power could
have gotten them in, and no one could get them
out. They had spent much time and money in
devil worship and sacrificing, hoping in that
way to get some peace. But things only grew
worse. Their husbands had heard at the meetings that Jesus Christ could cast out evil spirits,
and if this was true, they wanted to know what
they must do in order to get him to cast them out
of their homes. We sat down on the rug and

spent most of the afternoon reading the Scripture accounts of Christ's power over devils. And they were so glad to learn that 'He is the same yesterday, today and forever.' They learned also how the presence of the Holy Spirit in their homes would be a safeguard against the Evil One. It was not long before I heard that these women had given up all sacrificing and devil-worship, and were praying God to send the Holy Spirit to dwell with them. Soon they came to tell me that their homes were all peaceful. No more strange sights or sounds. No more sorcerers or exorcists. No more fear or devil-worship. But such joy and happiness as they had never known. They and their neighbors were filled with awe and wonder and wanted me to come and teach them more about the Holy Spirit and Jesus."

Let me say, in closing this chapter, that it is easy for us as Westerners to ridicule the superstitions of the Koreans; but if we, in a spirit of sympathy, assume for a time their angle of vision, we can see that to them the fear of demons is the cause of frequent and intense mental suffering.

CHAPTER IX

AN ADVENTURE ON THE HAN RIVER

It was at the time of the year when the streets of Seoul were resplendent with little children adorned, like Joseph of old, in "coats of many colors." It was the time when their elders, clad in new garments of spotless white, went about visiting their friends with Oriental effusiveness of respect, and at the same time contracted indigestion from eating so-called rice "bread" of the consistency of putty. In short, it was the Korean New Year season of the year 1889. At perhaps four o'clock of one bright, mild February afternoon I strolled up to the dispensary at Dr. Heron's house. The doctor's salutation was: "Gifford, don't you want to go hunting at the river?" Now I am so uncertain a huntsman that the ducks all laugh when they see me coming with a gun. I saw little use of my going upon a hunt. But a glance at the doctor's tired face changed my mind. The doctor was a man of such professional conscientiousness that he little knew how to spare himself. He had a dispensary at his home, where he saw Koreans and foreigners in the mornings; he was surgeon in charge of the royal government hospital, where he spent his after-

noons; he was physician to his majesty, liable to
calls at all hours; and added to this, he had
charge of the entire foreign practice of Seoul.
His wife was then an invalid, confined to her bed,
and much of the care of the Presbyterian Mission,
then in its day of beginnings, rested upon his
shoulders. Yes, I would go with him, but to
skate, not to hunt. Two white horses were called
up, one which the doctor had purchased for his
wife, and the other a loan to him from the king's
stables, for the doctor had a Tennesseean's fond-
ness for horses. Two servants carried our accou-
trements.

A pleasant ride brought us to the vicinity of
Yong-san upon the river's bank. Instead of
pausing here, however, we rode still farther up
the river to a cluster of houses where lumber is
cut and timbers prepared, conspicuous from the
distance for a goodly tiled house and a clump of
splendid great beech trees. Arrived here the
view was fine. Downward to the steamer landing
the river swept, with a bank that was a perfect
curve. In the background rose the bluff, man-
tled to the very top with the populous village of
Yong-san, in the center of which, like a bright
clasp, was set the red-brick Catholic Seminary.

We were soon off our horses. The winter had
been mild, and to my disappointment such ice as
remained on the river looked too fragile for skating. The interest therefore all centered in the
hunt.

There is a place near here in the river, especially where the river bends, the surface of which, even in the coldest winters when the ice in other places has been eight or more inches thick, I have never seen frozen over. Warm springs in the river doubtless account for this; and here, all winter long, waterfowls are feeding. At the water's edge below us was a row of large boats; beyond was a shell of thin ice, and still beyond was open water. In this open water was a succession of groups of wild swans, ranged down the stream like the links of a chain. One group in particular was not far away; and the doctor, eager for a shot, threw off his overcoat, which he replaced with a "turimachi," or long white outer-garment borrowed from a Korean. While I hid myself behind a pile of brush, he craftily sauntered down to the water's edge, in the hope that the birds might mistake him for an innocent-minded native puttering among the boats. But no, the swans, turning their graceful necks, gazed warily at the doctor, and, taking alarm, quickly glided out of range. But the doctor was a man of spirit, and was not so easily to be outdone. Presently he was hard at work, tugging at this great boat, shoving that one with all his might. But his efforts were in vain. The tide, so powerful along the coasts of Korea, was low in the river, and the boats could not be floated; and in addition, most of them were partly embedded in ice. A few moments later the doctor, some distance

away, has found a skiff. He motions for me to
come. The boat is made of pine boards clumsily
tacked together. We have no business to enter it.
But the fever of the hunt is upon us, and we are
not disposed to be critical. In we clamber,
followed by two half-grown boys to row us. The
doctor's handsome black dog sprang into the
water to follow us, but gesticulations and splash-
ings of the water induced her to swim back to the
shore. And now we are rapidly approaching the
flock that eluded us, the doctor in the prow and the
two lads erect and swaying to and fro as they
impel the boat by sculling in the peculiar native
fashion. Hope is vivid; but the wily swans, too,
are alert. They raise together, their pon-
derous wings pounding the water, and take their
flight to soar into the upper air. Failure only
urges the doctor on to seek the next flock farther
down the river. This flock, on being approached,
similarly took to flight; and the third, fourth,
and fifth flocks followed their example. Lastly
three or four ducks were started, and these, flying
somewhat nearer to our boat, the doctor ventured to fire at them, though I believe without
disastrous effect upon the birds.

Then simultaneously the thought occurred to us
both, "It is almost time for the gates to close."
In those ante-bellum days, every night shortly
after sundown, with a bray of horns and boom
of base-drum, the guardians of the city's peace
caused the great gates of the city to be closed,

and then retired to rest in the comforting delusion that all had been done that was necessary to keep out of the capital any hostile foe, even were he trained according to Western military methods—a system, indeed, of about as much practical efficacy as if a council of lambs should decide to ward off the attacks of wolves by the defensive use of their heels. The closing of the gates, with certain other ancient and interesting customs, has now passed out of vogue, to be sure, but in those days it was certainly no joke for the belated foreigner to find himself confronted of an evening by the closed leaves of two great, folding, iron-clad gates. It involved the staying outside the city all night, or climbing the high, slippery wall; but, be it whispered, the occasional jingle of a string of cash operated like magic in swinging open the portals, just as it was currently rumored, though of course most slanderously, that a similar jingle, only in greater volume, opened in the same magic way doors leading to rank and place in the governmental world. In a word, we little relished the idea of climbing the city wall after dark.

We must hurry. We could see the servants and horses on the shore, but could we get to them? A long field of ice lay between us and the bank. There was nothing to do but to row back up the river to our starting-place. The boys were not rowing fast enough. We took the oar in turn and rowed after the foreign fashion. But the oar

being peculiar our efforts were clumsy, and not
unlikely the wrenching of the boat resulting
therefrom started the seams. Of a sudden we
became aware that considerable water had come
in through the bottom. By this time the boys
were rowing. We observe that the water is
coming in much faster. The boys are now swinging at the sculling-oar with all their strength,
and with the prow headed for the ice. Now
and again, in their frantic endeavors, they drive
the boat into the ice, and the seams are opened
wider. Higher, higher creeps the water. Then,
in a moment I can never forget, I see the prow
pause for a moment, then sink out of sight under
the black, cold water. Neither of us could swim.
In a moment down we all went. It all happened
in less time than suffices for the telling. My
thought, as I sank, was to grasp at the boat
when I came to the surface.

And now this is our situation. We are on a
sand-bar in the very middle of the river. I am
standing in water up to my waist; the doctor is
in water up to his arm-pits, while only the heads
of the boys are visible. Natives told us afterward
that only a few feet on either side of where we
sank the water was deep enough to have drowned
us. Fortunately we were close to the ice. The
doctor was presently clambering out, his gun still
firmly grasped in his hand. Next, the boys were
trying in vain to leap out of the water. They were
in my way, as I came to where they clung at the

edge of the ice. So I reached down till I could grasp their baggy trousers and heaved them on like logs, and presently we were all upon the ice.

A glance at the ice-field was not reassuring. It was shell-ice with black air-holes all about us. Our location was about half-way between Yong-san and the hamlet with the beech trees. Those on shore were aware of our peril. In after days, when we could think of our misfortunes with greater cheerfulness, the doctor, with that peculiar, half-satirical twitch of his heavily mustached upper lip, would tell of the tremulousness of my tones as I called "*Ossa, ossa*" (hurry, hurry), and I believe I responded that his voice had taken on a hoarseness that was hardly natural. But if we are frightened, the boys are terrified. One is dancing about in a way that threatens to break the ice. Expostulations are unheeded. Only one thing remains: the doctor points his empty gun at the frantic youth, with the command to desist. Now force is an argument the validity of which, from centuries of use, the average Korean is prompt to recognize. The boy subsides. Soon quiet settles upon our group as we recognize that the men on shore are doing all that can be done, and that we dare not move about for fear of breaking the thin ice. The doctor, in his white Korean coat, sits upon the ice with his gun across his lap; I am kneeling with my overcoat tucked under my knees; one boy is standing erect and the other lad is seated. Night has now fallen, and from the overclouded sky the full moon sheds a dim and hazy light. Not a ripple stirs the water, and a deep quiet rests upon the river. True, we hear faintly, from the hamlet with the beech trees, the hum of voices, and sounds that suggest the chopping of ice around the ice-bound boats. As silent and motionless as a group of statuary, we keep our several attitudes for the space of an hour. The mental tension is extreme.

Finally we observe that water to the depth of an inch has come over the ice. The tide is coming in! Now the water has risen to the depth of two or three inches. Then we are conscious that the cake upon which we are seated has broken loose from the ice-field, and is turning around, preparatory to floating down the river. Our danger now is great, for should our frail raft strike against an obstruction, we would inevitably sink beneath the deep black waters.

But just then from an unobserved quarter, the direction of the village of Yong-san, came the sound of the plash of an oar. Through the dim moonlight we discern a boat with five rescuers approaching. The revulsion of feeling was strong. But still we dreaded lest, by the ungentle striking of the boat against the ice, we should be precipitated into the stream. Under the doctor's directions they reach the edge of the ice without mishap. A long oar is extended toward us, which we, beginning with the boys, grasp each in turn, and, sliding, are pulled to the edge of the boat and thus rescued. What ecstatic joy fills our hearts!

Upon reaching terra firma, the servants bring the horses. But to ride to Seoul from Yong-san in our frozen garments is out of the question. The doctor, full of resource, at once calls for Korean clothes. They are soon brought. We do not stop to enter a house, but under the dim moonlight, in an apartment walled about with living heads, we take off such garments as are wet or stiffened with ice, and replace them with the baggy Korean clothes, even to the straw sandals. The thought of the doctor's sick wife at home lends wings to his speed. In a moment he is ready and off on his horse. Our wet clothes are slapped together promiscuously upon a carrier's frame, and are started ahead upon the back of a coolie. Formal thanks to our benefactors are reserved for a later time and a form more substantial than words. Now, with the servant running beside, I set out at a rapid gait for the city, which brings again the glow of warmth into my frozen limbs.

Arrived at the city wall, the horse and servant must stay outside until the morning; and there is nothing for me to do but to clamber up the twenty feet of sheer stone wall. A man sent by the doctor is waiting to accompany me over the wall. Side by side he climbs with me, now drawing back my Korean robe so that I shall not be impeded, now guiding my hands to safe projections. Near the top he hastens ahead and pulls me over the wall. Thence a short, brisk walk brings me to the doctor's home, where I find him already arrived and clothed in his usual attire. Congratulations alternate with merriment at my appearance, while underneath it all was deep thankfulness for the Providence that had rescued us from peril. The next morning the servants who had accompanied us remarked that we were "as men who had come back from the dead." And I think they were correct. Two or three days later the two boys came to see us, and they reported that their mother, instead of rendering thanks to such deities as she knew, had soundly trounced them both, though for what reason they did not state. But as we fed them with Korean sweetmeats and gave them a proper amount of cash, I think that we consoled them.

CHAPTER X

With the exception of Thibet, which has its missionaries, yet keeps them barred beyond closed gates, Korea is the youngest of the missionary countries. Rev. John Ross, of Moukden, although a missionary to the Chinese in Manchuria, prior to the time of the signing of the treaties, became very much interested in the people of Korea through men of that land whom he met in Moukden, and who were able to converse with him through written Chinese. With the information thus acquired, he wrote a book in 1880, entitled "Corea, its History, Manners and Customs." He also employed some of these men to translate the entire New Testament into the Unmun. As a pioneer version it was good; but it would have been more available for use among the common people had Mr. Ross himself been personally acquainted with the language, so as to supervise the work of his Korean translators. His very great interest in the people was still further shown by his sending across the border into the north of the country Korean colporteurs with books; one of whose number, Mr. Saw, started the now flourishing work at Chang-yen in the Whang-Hai province, and later became one of the most valued helpers our Presbyterian mission has ever possessed.

The American Protestant missionary authorities were prompt to avail themselves of the opportunity, afforded them by the signing of the treaty in 1882, to enter the "Forbidden Land." In the spring of 1884, J. W. Heron, M.D., received appointment from the Northern Presbyterian Board to go to Korea. His departure, however, was delayed. In the summer of the same year Rev. Dr. R. S. McClay, of the Japan Methodist Conference, made a flying visit to Korea to spy out the land. The first Protestant missionary, however, to enter the country with the view to permanent abode was Dr. H. N. Allen, our present U. S. Minister to Korea, who, with his family, was transferred by the Presbyterian Board from China to Korea in the autumn of 1884. In a country where the martyrdom of the French fathers and thousands of their fellows was still fresh in the memory, and where the prejudice against all Western religions was still strong, the Doctor found it convenient to lay more emphasis on the fact that he was the physician of the foreign legations than that he had come with the view to opening Protestant missionary work. Dr. Allen's judiciousness, together with the éclat given him by the royal favor, which was due to his successful surgical treatment of the sword-cuts inflicted upon Min Yong Ik, a cousin of the queen, in the troubles of 1884, and which resulted in his

appointment as royal physician and surgeon in
charge of the government hospital, no doubt
materially smoothed the way for the labors of his
clerical brethren who shortly followed him.   In a
very material way it may be said that the gates
which long had been shut against the missionary
worker were opened at the point of a lancet.   In
the spring of 1885, Rev. H. G. Underwood, of the
Presbyterian Mission, who had   spent   several
months in Japan studying the Korean language,
appeared upon the scene.   He was known by the
authorities to be a clergyman, and as no objection
to his coming was raised by them, he was followed
in the summer by W. B. Scranton, M.D., and
family, and Rev. and Mrs. H. G. Appenzeller of
the M. E. Mission.   Soon after came J. W.
Heron, M.D., and wife, and presently Mrs. M.
F. Scranton appeared to join her son and enter
upon school and women's work.   The reception
afforded by the nobility and common people alike
to these "visitors from the West," who had
brought with them their wives and their belong-
ings, was an interesting compound of curiosity
and courtesy.   The missionary, meanwhile, was
left to quietly push his work.   That no conservative reaction should result, however, was more
than could be expected.   In 1888 the ancient
canard, that has made so much trouble in China,
that the missionaries were stealing and killing
babies for medicinal purposes, created a temporary disturbance in Seoul; and about this time the

authorities sought to restrict the so-called "proselyting" done by the missionaries. It raised a difficult question of conscience for us workers on the field. No one thought seriously of abandoning our religious work. Some believed that, like Peter and John under similar circumstances, they should appeal to a "higher law"; while others thought it the part of wisdom to bend temporarily before the storm, and pursue for a time "quieter methods," such, for instance, as the omission of the singing of hymns from the order of the church services. A year passed away, and scarcely a ripple remained to tell of the once perturbed waters. Unmolested, the work went steadily and strongly forward, with little of external history to record, until the spring of the year of the war, when there occurred the persecution of the Christians at Pyeng-yang, to be narrated in another chapter. In October, 1895, occurred the Decennial of the Founding of Protestant Missions in Korea, upon which occasion a number of important papers were read.

It should here be observed that, in addition to the two missions already mentioned, during the course of the years other sister missions came to their side, to join in the battle against heathenism. In 1889 came Presbyterian missionaries from far Australia; also in the same year Mr. M. C. Fenwick, of Canada, of the "Korean Itinerant Mission." In 1890, the genial Bishop F. J. C. Corfe arrived from England, with the representatives of the Society for the Propagation of the Gospel. In the same year appeared Dr. and Mrs. R. A. Hardie, of the Y. M. C. A. mission of Canada. In 1892 came our brothers of the Southern Presbyterian Mission. In 1895 appeared representatives of the training-school founded by the late Dr. Gordon, of Boston. Their official title is the "Ella Thing Memorial Mission," and they are Baptist in belief. In 1896, Rev. Dr. C. F. Reid, the well-known Chinese missionary, came as the advance-guard of the American Methodist Mission, South.

We have a roll of honor in Korea—those who have been summoned to a higher service and a richer life in the realm beyond the grave. There was Miss Anna P. Jacobsen, the trained nurse, with all the splendid fire and courage of her Viking ancestry; and Hugh Brown, M.D., full of sturdy strength; and John W. Heron, M.D., the soul of fidelity and honor—one whom all his friends loved as strongly as a blood relation. These were members of the Northern Presbyterian Mission. There was also the Australian Presbyterian missionary, Rev. John Henry Davies, who gave the promise of becoming the best all-round missionary in the land; and the tall, swarthy Presbyterian brother from Nova Scotia, Rev. William J. McKenzie, the successful advocate of native self-support; also William J. Hall, M.D., of the Northern Methodist Mission, the saintliest man that ever crossed the shores of Korea.

A Member of the Official Class.

There has always been a marked spirit of comity among the missionaries of Korea. The Methodist and Presbyterian missions, founded at about the same time, grew up together like two children. They had much the same experiences, and in a number of ways they united their work. The missions coming into the field at a later period imbibed the same fraternal spirit; and the whole work has thus far been conducted along the lines of certain well-marked, though unwritten, rules of comity. While the policy of the missions was still in a formative state, it was impossible for all to see eye to eye, but in those days the lines of cleavage ran nowhere near to the denominational walls. For instance, this was the case at the time when we were threatened with the transplantation of the "term question" to Korea. This controversy originated two hundred years ago between the Jesuit and Dominican missionaries in China. When the Protestant missionaries came, they took up the controversy where the others had left off, and for forty years their scholars argued the question. They may be at it yet, for aught that I know to the contrary. The question is simply this: the Chinese, and the Koreans too, recognize a supreme deity who, by the Chinese, is called Shangti and by the Koreans, Hananim, and of whom their conceptions are pure, though very vague. The term question, then, consists in whether or not it is allowable to adopt as the name for God the term Shangti, or

Hananim, and explain our conception of Him by the attributes we affirm of God. In Korea, rather than bequeath to our posterity an endless debate, the solution of the whole matter at which we arrived was that we cease to look for uniformity, and allow each person to use whatever one of half a dozen available terms he preferred.

The first ten years of mission work, terminating in 1894, the year of the war, was a period of preparation. We were learning Korean, and, what is still more important, Koreans. The preparation of a Christian literature had to be begun. We had all the difficulties that usually attend the process of getting our religion rooted in a new heathen soil. The people at large were invariably suspicious of us and our religion. Now and then whole groups of men would show an interest in our preaching; but because perhaps their mercenary aims had not been satisfied, or perhaps they lacked the moral courage to abandon their vices and heathen practices, their interest was not permanent. But, on the other hand, there were individuals and there were communities where the Gospel wrought a marked change in lives. Such converts, under careful Bible training, developed into excellent workers. Then came the war, and since then, beginning with the province in which Seoul is located and stretching away to the northern frontier, on the western side of the peninsula, there is a section of country where a marked forward religious movement has

been in progress, and in which the active agents
have been largely the Korean Christians themselves.

CHAPTER XI

Some people are of the opinion that anyone will do for a foreign missionary. Let us see. I have sometimes thought that, considering the expert knowledge which his circumstances from time to time require of the worker in foreign lands, that to be *ideally prepared*, the new missionary would reach his field of labor at the age of sixty years. In the first place, he must have a thorough collegiate education; and then he certainly must secure his diploma from the theological seminary. After this, he might take a year or two of study in the English Bible. And then, considering how well the art of the physician prepares the way for the acceptance of the message of the preacher, he might take a course in the medical college. Again, in the assignment of work, he is liable to be put in charge of a boys' school or "missionary college"; and who thinks of teaching school in these days of improved methods without a course of study in some normal school? For his translation work, he must be a trained linguist. Again, the native Christians are constantly bringing to him new and intricate questions, soliciting his advice, and the administrative work, which takes

so much of his time likewise calls for a judicially
trained mind; see how he would be benefited by
a course at the law school! In preaching to the
unconverted his audience is not composed of
intelligent heathen, as at home, but of heathen
densely ignorant of the Gospel; how, then,
should he know the most effective methods for
evangelistic preaching? From the number of his
native converts promising young men must be
selected and trained into preachers of the Gospel;
what an advantage to him to fill a professorship
in a theological seminary for a time! Then he is
liable to be made a treasurer of his mission or
station; several years' service as a bookkeeper in
a bank would splendidly fit him for his position.
Moreover, houses must be built, and the chief
business of the native carpenter is to cheat him
by day and by night, so perforce the missionary
becomes his own contractor. How could the
prospective missionary better fit himself for a
very necessary part of his work, than by driving
nails through an apprenticeship under a competent builder? Again, the zeal of the contributors
at home must be fed with the fuel of a constant
stream of journalistic articles from the pen of the
man on the field; a period of training as reporter
on the "Daily Hustler" would give him just the
literary style required for this portion of his
work. But, to speak in all seriousness, no moral
nor intellectual weakling will do for a foreign
missionary; and the more thorough his train-

ing and the broader his experience, the better are his chances of success.

Let me here quote the admirable missionary qualifications named by Dr. George Smith, at the convention of Student Volunteers, at Keswick, England, in July of 1893:

1. He should be conscious of the call of Christ and the gift of the Spirit.

2. He should covet earnestly the possession of the highest efficiency.

3. He must follow fully the rule of Christian charity and good temper.

4. He must learn habits of order and business ability, that will make him a wise steward of his Lord's money.

5. He must be sympathetic and loving toward native graces.

6. He must give himself to unceasing prayer.

7. He must yield absolute submission to the mind and will of God.

Allow me to add one word more; he must possess unquenchable patience.

With what interest do we look forward to the coming of the new missionary. We expect him to settle off-hand the questions that have perplexed us for years, upon the mere statement of the difficulty. But, strange to remark, the Presbyterian Board in New York places such a value upon his judgment that it will not let him vote until he has lived for a year upon the field; and its Korea mission has added the further requirement, that he can then vote only after having passed successfully his first year's examination in the language. I shall always remember the reply of that prince of missionaries, the lamented Rev. Dr. J. L. Nevius, of Chefoo, when, in answer to a query of mine relating to some question of mission policy in the conduct of schools, he replied: "If you had asked me that question twenty years ago, I could have told you. Now I do not know." In passing, let me pay a deserved tribute to the memory of that great and good man. In the spring of 1890, in the days when we, too, of the Presbyterian Mission in Korea, were "young missionaries," Dr. and Mrs. Nevius paid a visit to Seoul; and they so won our eager attention with their loving and wise counsels, that, as the result of their visit, our entire mission policy was altered for the better.

We come now to organization. In Korea, two types of mission organization prevail. In one type all the authority and power are vested in one man, the bishop. Such are the Roman Catholic and English Church missions. The Methodist Mission would probably come under this class, for certainly the Northern Methodist Mission is visited yearly by a bishop from America, who holds an annual conference and settles all important questions of mission policy. A number of the bishops, I may remark, have endeared themselves to the members of the foreign community in Seoul by holding meetings open to the general public, for the deepening of religious life. In the intervals between visits, the authority resides largely in a mission superintendent appointed by the bishop, though considerable power adheres in the general body of workers. The other type of organization is that of control by the mission itself, as exemplified in the Baptist and Presbyterian missions. In the matter of church organization, to assist in the oversight of the native work, our Methodist brethren are accustomed to license yearly Korean local preachers and exhorters. In the matter of church membership, they have two classes, full members and probationers, with the further distinction that some adult applicants receive baptism and some do not, while in a state of probation.

The Northern, Southern, and Australian Presbyterian missions of Korea, with an independent Canadian missionary, have combined their native work under one church organization, to which they have given the general name of "Jesus Doctrine Church." The male members of these missions are organized into a "Council of Presbyterian Missionaries," which is the highest church court we possess. In time this body will be transformed into a presbytery, or synod, when our Korean brethren become eligible for membership, for as yet we have no ordained native ministers and only one ruling elder. In a number of churches Korean deacons have been ordained, and in the course of time the other orders of

church officers will be set apart for their responsible positions. In our entire church government
we have what might be termed a preliminary
organization. In localities where missionaries
reside the churches are governed by foreign
sessions, in which the Korean deacons have a
seat, with the privileges of the floor, but no vote.
The work in the country districts is organized
along the line of the so-called Nevius system.
From the circle of believers in a given village are
chosen one or two of the most suitable men, who
are called "leaders," to whom are assigned the care
of the church services and the oversight of the believers, but without the power to administer the
sacraments. The West Gate Church of Seoul and
the church in the city of Pyeng-yang have both
a foreign session and a body of Korean leaders.

The country churches are visited periodically
by the missionary in charge, or his Korean
helper. Once a year a training-class is held at the
mission station, and the missionary invites these
leaders up for a term of study in the Bible. In
the taking of members into the church, we find it
wise to use the utmost caution. When the session,
or itinerating minister with sessional powers,
feels reasonably sure that a given person is a
Christian, then, with certain public ceremonies in
the church, the man is enrolled as a "catechumen,"
or applicant for baptism. He thereupon joins the
catechumen class, with a prescribed course of
study in the Bible and certain Christian books.

The general rule is that he wait at least six months before he be given church membership. The sessional examinations for admission to the church—I can speak with certainty for Seoul—are made very thorough, something between the similar examination of candidates in the home-land and the ordeal through which the young minister passes when examined by his presbytery for the licensure to preach. If the session feels satisfied with the examination, he is baptized and taken into the church; if the contrary is the case, he is asked to wait for a time, until his grasp of the truth is clearer, or, for instance, until he keeps the Sabbath better or attends with regularity the mid-week prayer-meeting.

Let us turn our attention to the work of the medical missionary. There is no doubt that in the early days of our Protestant missionary work in Korea, the doctor and the teacher, but more especially the doctor, did a preliminary work which made possible the labors of their clerical brethren. Let us watch a day's work in the Presbyterian hospital, under the charge of Dr. O. R. Avison, in the buildings kindly loaned to the mission by his majesty, who has in many ways shown his appreciation of the missionaries' aim and work, as when, in an audience he accorded to Bishop Ninde, of the Methodist church, early in 1895, he directly requested him to send more missionaries. In the wards each morning, prayers, with a suitable amount of religious teaching,

are conducted by the doctor.   There is a pay
ward and a general ward.   The foreign lady
nurse, with the aid of a corps of three or four
bright-faced Korean hospital assistants, attends to
the dressings of the patients.   Perhaps a surgical
operation is on hand, over in the large operating
room, when the entire force must be present; or
the doctor calls the young fellows above mentioned, who are also studying medicine with him,
into his room for a medical lecture.   The afternoon comes, and a group of men are seen outside
in the court or in the room provided for them,
waiting for the dispensary to open.   A little bell
tinkles, and a man holding a strip of wood in his
hands, on which is marked a given number in
Chinese characters, arises and goes within to the
doctor, to be followed shortly by the man with the
next higher number.   Presently, a clerical missionary or Korean helper joins the waiting group
to tell them that there is healing for their sin-sick
souls as well as for the ills of the body.   A Christian bookstore adjoins the waiting-room.   Tinkle,
tinkle, and another man goes inside.   Let us go
with him.   In the dispensary we find the doctor
and his assistants.   The cases are disposed of
systematically and rapidly.   The name of the man
and the nature of his trouble go into the register.
If it be medicine that is required, a prescription
is promptly written and passed in to the youth in
the drug room.   If a minor operation be necessary, the instruments swiftly do their work.   A

nominal charge covering the cost of the medicines is made in a number of the cases.   And so the afternoon passes in the effort to bring help to the bodies and souls of a few of this world's sick ones.

There is a women's department of the hospital, with a lady physician to meet the patients.   But, in considering this branch of the work, I am going to take you to the women's hospital of the Methodist Mission, in the center of the foreign settlement.   We find Doctor Mary M. Cutler in charge.   Her small, but well-appointed hospital nestles beside the street under the hill of the large girls' school.   In addition to Korean female assistants, some of whom are graduates of the school, she has the help of missionary workers, one a trained nurse and one a Bible worker. To the hospital come the women, some in closed chairs and some on foot.   Part of the work is done in the hospital, and part in the homes of the patients, and in both places we can be certain that the Gospel truth is faithfully taught.   The diseases the doctors meet with are chiefly malaria, indigestion, worms, skin diseases, eye troubles, bone and joint diseases, consumption, venereal diseases, smallpox, remittent fever, a species of typhus fever called *impiung*, and occasionally a leper is seen.   The native doctors have their herbs and mixtures, some of which are fairly good.   In their practice they frequently stick needles into the flesh, and apply the burning of the moxa to the skin; but of surgery they have absolutely no knowledge and it is here that the foreign doctor makes his reputation.

There is one sharp distinction between the heathen and the Christian spirit. The heathen helps his relative or the member of his guild or insurance society, who can be relied upon to help him in turn in the hour of need; but for the poor unfortunate whose only claim is the bond of a common humanity, he does absolutely nothing. On the other hand, the Christian, in the spirit of the Good Samaritan, not merely looks with compassion upon the suffering stranger, but cares for him as well, either as an individual or collectively by the erection of hospitals and asylums of every description. Here is an instance: A few years ago, at certain seasons of the year, both inside and outside of the west wall of Seoul, you might have seen numbers of the sick and dying stretched upon the ground. They were people afflicted with contagious diseases, servants or poor people occupying buildings in the compounds of more prosperous Koreans, who had cruelly turned them into the streets to die. This is, however, no longer the case; for Christian philanthropy has provided, outside the west gate of the city, the "Frederick Underwood Shelter," where the outcast sick may resort for shelter and medical care. In connection with this institution, Mrs. Dr. Underwood conducts a dispensary.

What an arsenal is to an army, such the mission press is to the band of missionary workers. The

Tri-lingual press of the Methodist Mission, founded by our large-hearted brother, the Rev. F. Ohlinger, now returned to his former field in Foochow, China, furnishes the American missionaries with the larger part of their missionary literature. They are able to print in English, Unmun or Chinese, whence the mission press gets its name. Without neglecting other forms of work, there is a considerable literary activity on the part of the missionaries. First and most important is Bible translation. Engaged in this work are the following Board of Bible Translators: Messrs. W. D. Reynolds, of the Southern Presbyterian Mission; H. G. Appenzeller and W. B. Scranton, of the Northern M. E. Mission; M. N. Trollope, of the English Church Mission; J. S. Gale and H. G. Underwood, representing the Northern Presbyterian Mission. They have translated the Gospels, Acts and about one half of the Pauline Epistles. When a translator has finished a given book of the Scriptures, he prepares a blankbook with vertically ruled columns, as many as there are translators, and in the right-hand columns he writes his own translation. The book is then handed around, and his colleagues write, in the columns assigned to them, their renderings of the text. It eventually returns to the translator, who prepares his final copy in the light of the suggestions of the others. The cost of publishing is borne by the American and the British and Foreign Bible societies. We are able to use to a limited extent Christian literature printed in Chinese, sent us from Shanghai, but for the use of the common people we are obliged to print in Unmun.

The Korean Religious Tract Society is another of our institutions, which is undenominational in character. This year it published some 37,000 books and leaflets. With the exception of a few sheet tracts, the publications of the society are sold by the missionaries, as a rule, at a nominal price. It is believed that thereby the books meet with better treatment. Many of the missionaries in active work have translated a book or two, but the most prolific translators are probably Mr. Gale and Dr. Underwood. Each has prepared a text-book and a dictionary, besides translating parts of the Scriptures. Mr. Gale also published, with funds raised by Rev. Dr. A. T. Pierson, a translation of Pilgrim's Progress; and Dr. Underwood has translated numerous tracts and hymns. The Korean *Repository*, published monthly in English, is a magazine that deals with Korean topics, some of a missionary character, but for the most part of a secular nature. The magazine has been commended by journals both in America and in the Far East for the bright, readable nature of its contents, much of the credit for which is due to the able editing of the Revs. H. G. Appenzeller and George Heber Jones, of the Methodist Mission. Two religious weekly newspapers printed in Unmun, the one the "Christian

News," edited by Drs. Underwood and C. C. Vinton, the other the "Christian Advocate," with Rev. Mr. Appenzeller for editor, came into being last winter.

I shall now ask my reader to draw upon his imagination a bit, and in fancy we shall step upon a magic carpet, like the enchanted objects of which you have read in the "Arabian Nights' Entertainments," and together we shall fly hither and thither about the country seeing how various kinds of evangelistic work are done by the different missionaries.   Let us drop in upon Miss Mattie Tate, of the Southern Presbyterian Mission at Chun-ju, in the South, and observe her in her women's work.   She has a room where she receives her Korean women visitors.   As we see her, she has a group of women about her, all sitting on the floor.   Many are old acquaintances; a few have come for the first time.   The elaborate introductions, with the inquisitive questions about age, etc., which they consider so polite, are now over.   The conversation has been turned to religious topics, and she is teaching them the truths of the dear old Bible.   Now one of the strangers breaks in with a question as to the texture of her foreign dress. Another one follows with a story of her troubles.   It is so hard for her, a widow woman, to live; and cannot the teacher help her?   But other heads, bent in serious thought, show that the spiritual words of the speaker have taken hold upon them, like the seed that fell on good ground in the parable of our Savior. The lady worker engaged in evangelistic labor among the women, a form of work which the men, by reason of the customs of the country, are unable to do, also visits in the home of the women. She conducts one or two regular classes of Bible study for their benefit during the week; sits with them on the women's side of the curtain at church, and occasionally gets into her "chair" (a box-like contrivance, composed of a frame and curtains, with a couple of parallel poles underneath for the benefit of the coolies that carry her), and with a Korean Bible woman she goes out to teach the women in country villages.

We will now drop down into Fusan to watch a winter training-class, such as Rev. W. M. Baird, of our mission, used to conduct there before his transfer to the more pressing work in the Pyeng-yang region. The teacher sits on the floor at the warm end of the room. Following Korean custom, certain men, who, on account of their birth or knowledge, consider themselves superior to the others, have seated themselves next to him. Each has before him a Chinese Testament or a Unmun Gospel. Some have in front of them a note-book, an ink-stone, a small stick of ink, and some little brushes to take notes. They are studying one of the Gospels. The exercise begins with a quiz on yesterday's lesson, and then the lecture on the new chapter follows. These "leaders," or if the work be less advanced, interesting inquirers from

the country villages, have been specially invited
to come up to the station for a month's or six
weeks' study, and while the class is in session are
entertained at mission expense. There are two
or three lectures a day, studying the Bible as a
whole or in parts, and the missionary gives his
whole strength to the class while it is in session.
All due attention is paid to exegesis, but the main
emphasis is laid upon those scriptural truths which
tend to deepen spiritual life and make aggressive
workers. Much prayer also attends the gathering
of the winter class, and we all feel that this form
of work is one of the most profitable in which we
can engage.

Let us next step off at Gensan, upon the east
coast of the country. We are in the native town.
It is a busy time of the day, and the streets present an ever-changing picture of animated life.
But before one little building is gathered the largest crowd. It is the street chapel of Rev. W. L.
Swallen, of our Presbyterian mission. This has
been his method of work: At a certain fixed hour
in the day he has ridden over on his wheel from
the foreign settlement. The windows and door
facing the street have been opened wide. Just
inside the door he and his helper, with possibly
another Christian or two, have taken their stand.
The old familiar strains of "Nearer, My God, to
Thee," and "What Can Wash Away My Sins?"
joined to not unmelodious Korean words, have
rung out upon the street. In a very few minutes

a crowd has gathered, curious to know the meaning of the unfamiliar sounds.   On being invited
in, they have speedily filled the room and throng
outside about the windows and door.   A word of
quiet prayer is uttered, and then the helper begins
an explanation.   They are the believers in a doctrine that puts into the heart a joy whose most
natural expression is song.   Then, to explain the
doctrine, he tells them of God and His attributes,
and how in His sight we all are sinners, and how
Christ died to take away our sin and makes us at
one with God.   The majority of a street chapel
audience are the rawest kind of heathen.   Their
creed might be summed up as follows: Get enough
to eat; get enough to wear; indulge all your
passions; honor your dead father; and keep the
devils from harming you.   They find it hard to
understand   our   Christian   terminology.   The
heathen Korean knows   the Supreme Being as
Hananim, the "Lord of Heaven," and he thinks
of Him vaguely as Providence, or God, as He is
revealed in Nature.   But that this Being takes
note of his good or evil deeds seems never to have
entered his head.   The devils he knows better.
The preacher speaks of "sin," and he thinks he
is speaking of a fault, a mistake or a civil crime.
That he should repent of his sins to God is to him
an entirely new thought.   He stumbles over the
atonement like   a   modern Unitarian.   The
preacher speaks of "love to God," and uses a term
containing a certain warmth; but the auditor

finds it hard to grasp the thought, because in heathen usage the Koreans have no term expressive of the love of an inferior for his superior, but only a word that denotes profound respect. So, in chapel-preaching, the speaker can take nothing for granted, but must repeatedly explain those fundamental truths which seem to us as clear as the statement that two and two make four. It is a form of preaching, too, that makes a man feel his utter personal weakness, and throws him back upon the power of God. The crowd in Mr. Swallen's chapel is quiet and attentive in the main; but it is hard to tell from the apathetic faces what impression is really being made upon their hearts. Now a drunken man creates a temporary disturbance. Then a man in the crowd, by a flippant jeer, raises a laugh which is quickly silenced by the mentally alert helper. Still another man asks a series of questions that show his honest desire to know the truth. The helper finally ceases, and Mr. Swallen and the Christians in turn succeed him in the "scattering broadcast of the seed upon the waters."

Now, upon the flying rug again, and we alight in one of the business streets of Seoul. Rev. E. C. Pauling, of the Baptist Mission, is standing quietly at one side of the street. Under his arm are a number of tracts and leaflets. He opens one and quietly reads to himself. Instantly a Korean head straightens up and looks at him. Its owner edges nearer. The foreigner seems to take no notice; yet to all appearance unconsciously he has begun to read aloud. This is too much for the curiosity of the Koreans along the street, and in a moment a crowd has gathered about him. This is his opportunity, and he begins to preach much as our friends in the street chapel did. His helper presently relieves him. And then they distribute a number of leaflets, and the helper sells some books. This street-preaching, too, is a form of the broadcast sowing of Gospel seed.

We now alight upon a commodious junk, going down the Han River from Seoul, with a boatman or two swaying from right to left at the great sculling-oar. In a cozy little cabin at one end of the boat we find Rev. S. F. Moore, of our Presbyterian Mission. He zealously devotes his entire time to one form or another of evangelistic work. He has done considerable work among the butchers, who occupy almost the lowest round in the Korean social ladder, and is now on his way down the river to visit his Christians in a number of villages scattered along the shore.

Now, to see another form of teaching, which we call "Sarang work," we will return to the North Chulla province in the south, this time to the seaside village of Kunsan. Rev. W. M. Junkin, of the Southern Presbyterian Mission, sits in his *sarang*, a thoroughly Korean room, where he sees his native guests. He and several Korean men sit on neatly woven mats of straw spread upon the comfortably heated floor. Mr. Junkin holds in his hand an Oxford Bible, and his helper has open before him a copy of the Chinese Scriptures, ready to render into the vernacular any passage he may indicate. Although the Chinese Bible is a sealed book to the common people, we missionaries, in our preaching and teaching, read it constantly to them through the eyes and lips of our helpers. An easy, pleasant conversation is apparently in progress. One man, with his hands clasped about his slightly elevated knees, in a mild excitement sits rocking to and fro as he talks. The animated discussion which we here behold has for its theme the claims of the doctrines of the Christian religion upon the belief of men. In connection with the *sarangs* and street chapels, a number of the missionaries have small Christian bookstores which are conducted by their helpers. Some Christian quinine-sellers also keep our books in stock.

Back again to Seoul we fly. Just as we pass through that magnificent piece of masonry, the South Gate of the city, we behold Dr. W. B. Scranton, the Superintendent of the Northern Methodist Mission, mounted on a bicycle. Behind him, led by a well-browned boy, smartly steps a Korean pony, sleigh-bells jingling at his neck, laden with a pack-saddle and a couple of evenly balanced boxes filled with an assortment of canned food, Christian books and clothing. Laid on top, between the boxes, is a bundle of bedding, with sundry parcels belonging to the Koreans of the party.   Not far behind, at a comfortable pace, swing along his Korean helper and cook.   The doctor is just starting out upon a country itinerating trip, to be gone for a month or six weeks.   In going to the country, some of the missionaries travel in the popular Korean way, on foot; some have a couple of light boxes fastened to the pony's pack-saddle, spread some blankets above, climb to the top and ride away, their feet dangling on either side the pony's neck, while the pony boy guides the craft; but perhaps the greater number use wheels.   The roads, I may say, are frequently narrow bridle-paths.   Some of us have found it profitable for a doctor and minister to travel together.   Dr. Vinton and myself, indeed, have joined forces in a number of itinerating tours.   The ladies sometimes make a similar combination; as, for instance, Mrs. Gifford with Miss G. E. Whiting, M.D.   We try to look upon our trips to the country as a kind of excursion, and so it would be if the pure air and fine scenery had the other things to match them.   But one finds it a little hard to carry out the illusion, for instance, when sleeping in a stuffy room with five varieties of vermin engaged in your vivisection, three or four of the bones in your anatomy protesting against the hardness of the hot, stony floor, and your mind conscious of the fact that the country is full of robber bands that have a way of visiting the villages when they are least expected.   This is mentioned here only to show that missionary labor, like every other form of work in this world, has, in addition to a great many pleasant features, a few things that one could wish were otherwise. The doctor, while on his country circuit, stops in each village where he has work—at the house of one of the Christians, for two or three days, not paying board, but making his host a "present" of money. The days and nights are busily filled, preaching to the unconverted, instructing the Christians, examining candidates and administering the sacraments. As in other lands, we consider that in the country villages we have perhaps our most hopeful field of effort.

Let us consider briefly the private life of the missionary. Wherever a group of missionaries (possibly belonging to different missions) live, they unite for the holding of religious services in English. Thus in Seoul we have an organization called the Union Church, which has a Sunday-afternoon preaching service conducted by the various ministers, in turn, in the chapel of the Pai-chai college of our Methodist brethren, and a Thursday-night prayer-meeting held in the different missionary homes. Where there is a foreign community of any size we are able to forget our mission problems and cares in an occasional gratification of our social natures. But the people in the far interior, with only one or two foreign families in the station, undoubtedly feel the loneliness of their voluntary exile among alien peoples.

The missionaries in Korea, as a rule, live with the same simplicity as ministers in the country villages of America, with the one exception that the customs of the country require them to keep, at low wages, two or three servants, the whole company of whom they would gladly exchange for one strong, competent Bridget or Gretchen. Remember, too, that this frees the missionary's wife to do a work among the women of her husband's church which he cannot do, or enables her to help the mission cause in some other direct way. In the matter of food, we can buy certain meats and some fruits and vegetables on the field, but we live for the most part out of tin cans and barrels, shipped perhaps twice a year from America. Our expensive fuel, burned in the stoves we have imported, consists of pine wood, a sooty Japanese coal, and bags of Korean hard coal, mostly dust, which latter we mix with clay and dry into coal-balls. A majority of the missionaries tithe their salaries for the benefit of the mission work, while some give a much larger proportion, especially in the days when our brethren in the home-land are derelict in their financial duty to the foreign-mission cause. In spite of the depressing influence of their constant contact with heathenism and their endless care of "babes in Christ," a number of the missionaries show a marked growth in spirituality.

A few words may be in order with reference to our Korean inquirers and converts. Perhaps due to the popular report that the French fathers, with whom the people continually confuse us, now and then interest themselves in the lawsuits of their converts, men seek to attach themselves to us as adherents, in the hope that by so doing they may secure the aid, in their civil cases before the magistrates, of the political influence which we, as foreigners, are supposed to possess. But, as they find that it is our mission policy not to take up such cases, their interest soon disappears. Be it noted, however, that occasionally men with such ulterior aims, or those whose real motive is the desire to get employment, develop into genuine inquirers as the Holy Spirit, through the Word of God, takes hold upon their hearts.

You may perhaps be under the impression that it is an easy thing for a Korean to become a Christian. If so, let me disabuse your mind. From the moment the man decides for Christ, a complete revolution in the tenor of his life begins. One of the great days for the worship of ancestors arrives, and on conscientious grounds he refuses to join in the worship. Immediately he finds himself in trouble, and this is especially true if he happens to belong to the *Yangban*, or aristocratic class, whose claims to social superiority depend so largely upon the universally strict adherence to the system of Confucius, who taught, as one of the "five relations," the division of all the people of the realm into two classes, the gentlemen and the "low fellow." To class pride is added a measure of superstitious fear. Hence our Christian finds himself opposed by the bitter anger of the men of his family, and all his near and distant relations, not to mention the dislike and ridicule of the rest of the community. If nearly all the members of the village happen to be his relatives, we can imagine his hard lot. Where a number of Christians live in the same neighborhood, of course the conditions are not so severe. One *Yangban* complained to me that giving up ancestral worship made it almost impossible for him to marry off his children in his own social class. The Christian decides to burn the implements of demon-worship. At once he is assailed by the tears and the imprecations of the female part of his household. Suppose, in the days of his heathen ignorance, he had contracted plural marriage relations. He now has a very delicate and painful duty to perform, in view of the church law, framed in America, which requires him to put away all his wives and offspring, except the first wife and her children. Then, as a man who refuses to follow the almost universal customs of drinking and gambling, he is considered "peculiar." If he is a merchant, Christian principle requires that he mend his ways to a course of strict honesty in his transactions; and that the step is a hard one, can be seen from the fact that the delusion is common among Koreans that the merchant who will not cheat and defraud cannot do business. Then, if the Christian has

been following a sinful occupation, or one of
doubtful morality, he must give it up.   The
observance of the Sabbath he also finds difficult
in a country where nearly every one lives from
hand to mouth, and all the rest of the community,
except the Christians, work or do business on
Sunday; and again, if he lives in the country,
where the fifth day market for his region falls
every now and then upon the Sabbath.   One of
his minor difficulties is mental confusion over the
denominational differences of the various missions, which differences, I may say, many of the
missionaries seek to minimize in their teaching.
He is troubled, too, with certain things in the
Scriptures, in a way peculiar to the Eastern mind.
For instance, in the parable of the unjust steward,
Luke, 16th chapter, taking a very literal view of
the shifty procedure of the man, which is just
what a Korean would have done under the circumstances, he is confused with what to him is
the moral paradox of the passage.

You may like to know what changes for the
better we see in the lives of the Korean Christians.   In view of the variations in character of
the church members in the home-land, it is super-
fluous that I tell you that we have weak Christians
and strong Christians.   The two great temptations
for our converts are to dishonesty and immorality,
and occasionally one will fall.   But, on the other
hand, I have known men to move away from
their native villages rather than resume the

ancestral worship.   Women who have passed from the bondage of the fear of demons to the joyous freedom they experience in the love of Christ, testify that they "feel relieved of such a burden"; and that "it is almost as though they were living in another world."   I know of homes that are happier.   The Korean brethren are quick to notice the more exalted place the wife occupies in the missionary home, with the result that their own wives get better treatment.

Drinking and other bad habits are abandoned. Men, for the sake of conscience, change their occupations.   For example, I remember one Christian man, whom I met in Pyeng-yang, who had formerly made an excellent profit from the painting of pictures to be used in heathen worship, but having given up the business from a sense of duty was at that time finding it difficult to live.   In Sabbath observance there is much improvement.   One young merchant, doing business on borrowed capital, had to return the money to its owner because he refused to keep open on Sunday.   But in his fidelity he was prospered, for he soon secured from another man the money to open across the street a still larger shop than the one he had lost for conscience sake.   In the native Christians who study their Bibles—and is it not true at home as well?—one can observe an ennobling of character that is perceptible even in the expression of their faces.   One occasionally sees revealed in them a simplicity of faith that is touching. In one region in the north the Christians confidently declare that, when the cholera was epidemic, as the result of prayer their families and in some cases their villages were spared when all about them the people were dying. According to their means, they are willing givers to the Lord. They are warmly patriotic. They take on readily an *esprit de corps* which makes them aggressive workers for the salvation of other Koreans. In the church services they are quiet and reverent. There is something wonderfully suggestive in the posture adopted by the Korean Christians in prayer. Sitting as they do on the floor of the church, when the time for prayer arrives they bow their bodies forward till the forehead or the hat-brim touches the floor. This is a form of Oriental prostration. The Oriental prostration suggests the thought not only of profound reverence, but of complete submission to the will of the superior. While in that position the superior can work what he will upon the humble form before him. My reader, is not that the mental attitude you and I ought to take before God—completely surrendered, that Jesus Christ may cleanse from the heart all its selfishness and sin, and fill the place thus made empty with His own blessed presence and the "more abundant life"?

CHAPTER XII

The following is the story told me by Mr. Moffett, which serves to illustrate once again the power of Christ's salvation to change the lives of men, whether their hue be yellow or white:

"When my helper, Mr. Han, first visited Pyeng-yang to begin the preliminary work of opening our station there, he took a stock of books and stopped at an inn kept by a Mr. Chay, who, besides being an inn-keeper, was also a broker, selling upon commission whatever goods his guests might bring. Mr. Han had known him some years, having formerly stopped there when traveling as a merchant. Han began preaching to all in the inn and selling the tracts. Chay was a tall, slender man, "hail fellow well met" with everyone, given to loud talking, drinking, gambling and a vicious life generally, always ready for a joke and yet addicted to loud quarreling with any and every one. As an inn-keeper and business man he was very shrewd and able, but was always wasting his earnings in wine, gambling and immorality, and he made his home very miserable. He liked Han and listened to the strange story he had to tell and wondered greatly

at his selling such nice-looking books at such a
low price. The truth, however, took not the
slightest hold upon him then, but simply because
Han was his guest, he used his influence to help
him sell the books, telling everyone that they
were good books. Later, when we visited Pyeng-
yang and sought to purchase property, Mr. Chay
acted as our agent and came into more intimate
contact with us, as we too made the Gospel our
daily subject of conversation. Mr. Saw, our
evangelist, who accompanied us, made a great
impression upon Mr. Chay, as he had never seen
a Korean who had the gentle spirit and the truth-
fulness which Mr. Saw displayed. Mr. Chay
attended the services we conducted on the Sabbath, not, as he has since said, that he cared at
all for the truth, but simply because, as our agent,
he wished to retain our goodwill. Contact with
the truth and with those who showed such earnest
zeal in proclaiming this truth, in spite of all the
ridicule and opposition heaped upon them, caused
him to begin to think, and then to listen, and then
to read, and, much to his surprise, he found himself really interested and concerned. The Spirit
of God took hold upon him and he became a daily
student of the Word of God, being one of the most
constant attendants upon the Sabbath services
and the catechumen class. He met with the
most abusive ridicule and insult, and he had the
finger of scorn constantly pointed at him as he
walked the street between his inn and the chapel.

Always an outspoken man, he met all this abuse
most bravely, and frankly confessed that he was
'doing the Jesus doctrine.' Old friends and com-
rades in evil conspired to make him again fall into
sin, visiting him and doing all they could to lead
him to gamble and drink.

"His wife was thoroughly enraged when he
refused to sacrifice to the evil spirits of the household, and she begged him to ward off the great
evils she feared because of his failure to placate
those evil spirits. He had, through his faith in
Christ, become indeed a 'new creature.' He
had given up his adultery, drunkenness and gambling, his fighting in the home and on the street,
and he had caused his home-coming, from day to
day, to become a pleasure to his wife and children, instead of a cause for fear. While his wife
rejoiced in all this, such was her fear of the evil
spirits that she was distressed and angry when he
not only refused to take part in the sacrifice, but
urged the throwing away of all the baskets and
bundles of straw which represented the abodes
of these evil spirits.

"He put to her this pointed question: 'Which
will you have me do: be a Christian and be as I
am, sober, loving and true to you, or worship
evil spirits, and get drunk, lead a vile life, gamble
and make my home-coming a terror to you and
the children?' Then she would plead with him
not to go back to his old habits, but yet to join in
the sacrifices. The poor woman did not know her

own mind.   One day she would bless Mr. Han and me, and call us her best friends, because of the great reform in her husband; the next day she would break out into the most bitter cursing, declaring that we had no business to come there and prevent her husband from offering sacrifice to the evil spirits and to his ancestors.   Mr. Chay's brothers, too, did not know just what position to take; they cursed him for leaving off the ancestral worship, but rejoiced in his reformation. For months he was subject to all kinds of temptations.   At times he fell.   But as he grew in knowledge of Christ, his faith became stronger, and it was touching to hear him tell of his going into the inner quarters of his house and kneeling in prayer for strength to resist the temptations which came upon him so often through the day. A touching incident may here be mentioned which will reveal also the difficulties with which the Korean Christians have to contend and likewise the gradual process by which they come to realize the sinfulness of sin, while at the same time it will show how their habits are so fastened upon them that they do not realize the possibility of leading an entirely holy life:

"One day he came rushing into my room, not far from his inn, saying that he had just run away from a crowd of his former friends who were trying to make him drink.   First he told them he was not well; but they would not listen to that. Then he said it would make him sick to drink, as his stomach was paining him; but this they regarded as no excuse. Then he said he was now a Christian and could not drink. But with that they seized him by the hair and, ridiculing him and abusing him for adopting the foreign religion, attempted to make him drink with them as of old. He at last agreed, but said he had an engagement just then and would be back in a few minutes to drink with them. Rushing out, he came into my room, telling me of the occurrence and the way in which he had gotten away from them and avoided drinking. I rejoiced with him in his determination not to yield, but called his attention to the fact that he had lied to them and that he must not commit one sin in order to avoid another. He looked very queer and quickly exclaimed: 'Oh! I have got to lie.' Then I showed him the sinfulness of lying and, again, looking very queer as the realization of the sin came over him, in connection with his own conviction that he could never get away from his old evil habits without lying, he exclaimed: 'Well, it *is* wrong to lie; and I will quit after New Years. But I *must* lie until then.' Mr. Chay was one of the first seven men received into the church in Pyeng-yang and has since then become constantly more interested and has lived an increasingly consistent life, contributing liberally and working most zealously to make known to others the truth which has done so much for him. He places Christian books in his inn and urges all guests to read and buy, and wherever he goes in the city or surrounding country, he constantly invites friends and acquaintances to listen to the Gospel. His influence in his own family constantly grew, although they, at the time of the persecution, when he was arrested, bound with the red cord used for tying criminals and threatened with death, as well as afterward, when an official, who was a friend of the family, called him privately and warned him to give up Christianity upon fear of death, again greatly urged him to give up his belief or flee. When the threats of persecution were renewed, he and another of the Christians fled to the country and, after wandering around for one whole night in the rain, in constant dread lest at any point on the road they might meet an officer seeking their arrest, they talked the matter over and Mr. Chay said: 'Here! If God intends that we shall die, we cannot escape by fleeing. We might as well go back and take whatever comes, leaving it all to Him.' The next day they returned, came in to see me and said to the little band of Christians, who knew of their flight, that they were ready to give a reason for the faith that was in them and to take the consequences. The war came on and Mr. Chay took all his family and that of his brother to a mountain village, where he made known the truth very clearly, and where his own faith and peaceful life in the midst of trouble and threatening gloom brought his older brother and his wife to a saving faith in Christ.   His wife, having lost all her desire to worship the evil spirits and continue the ancestral sacrifices, formed one of the first groups of women to be received into the church after Mrs. Lee joined the station.   In the mountain village where they took refuge there are now fifteen or more Christians meeting every Sunday, although Mr. Chay and his family have long since returned to the city.

"Mr. Chay is one of the best-known Christians in Pyeng-yang, and his marked reformation has done much to commend the Gospel to the people of that vicinity."

CHAPTER XIII

The scope of this chapter will deal with a variety of educational institutions that flourish within the sweep of the mediæval walls of Seoul, which fall like widely draped festoons from the peaks of the North and South mountains. Imagine yourself, please, in a factory where a planing-machine and three or four circular saws are tearing the air into shreds with their din. You can then form some conception of the noise of a native Korean schoolroom when the pupils are conning their lessons. Let us take a look into such a school. Perhaps a dozen bright-faced lads are sitting cross-legged upon the floor, their Chinese books laid before them. The upper parts of their bodies are swaying violently, each with his own time and motion, some from side to side, others forward and back, and all of them vociferating, in every pitch of voice, the lesson assigned for the day. In contrast with all this movement and din is the quiet form of the school-master, sitting at the end of the room where the flue-heated floor is the warmest, on his head a crown-shaped, horse-hair hat, his nose surmounted by a pair of scholarly goggles, with a book before him, and in his hand a rod; and now and again his stentorian tones mingle with the shrill trebles as he hurls in a word or two of correction. This is the ordinary Korean school.

From early dawn till the sun goes down these lads drone away, now studying aloud, now writing the characters, now reciting to the master the contents of the Chinese classics, filled with the lore of the ancient sages and a pseudo-history, but with scarcely an idea to lead them to understand the world in which they live in the present year of Our Lord.

Anyone who knows the Korean people, even in the most superficial manner, must be aware that there is something radically lacking in the time-honored system of education of the country.

I would by no means condemn it as an utter failure. Let no one beguile himself into thinking that the educated Koreans are a dull class of people. The study of the Chinese classics has much the same educational value for the Korean that a classical course in Latin and Greek has for a student in the Occident. The effort to master the difficult language is in itself a mental discipline. The writings of Confucius and Mencius, as a system of mere ethics, together with much that is defective and a disproportioned stress laid upon the virtue of filial piety, contain also much that is undoubtedly beautiful and true. Then again, to such an extent have the Chinese words and phrases imbedded themselves in the native speech, that no Korean can obtain a mastery of his own language without a preliminary study of the Chinese. But, when all has been said, the popular education of Korea leaves very much to be desired. The best way to judge of a system is to examine the finished product of that system. Let us consider, then, the average educated Korean. He has a certain mental brightness and polish. His memory is noticeably well trained. He seems, indeed, to be much like a mill fairly well fitted to grind, but with no worthy content upon which to grind. He has, in a measure, the intellectual power of a man, with the actual knowledge of a child. And the discouraging feature of his case is that he has, in many instances, become so self-conceited that Socrates himself could not convince him of his ignorance. He is color-blind to everything modern. His eyes are set on the past, especially the Chinese past. He is a slave to the traditions and customs transmitted from antiquity. His thinking has no breadth nor originality. But the fault is moral as well. Among people of his own station in life he displays a ceremonious politeness that is certainly charming But do not for a moment be deceived. There is very little heart in it. What Korean unreservedly trusts another Korean? And for the man below him in social rank he has all the contempt of a Brahmin. Again, he has a false pride which leads him to starve rather than do a stroke of honest manual labor. The ruling principle of his life is

A Gentleman of the Old School.

apt to be a selfish individualism, which leaves in
his heart but little room for a disinterested public
spirit, or a true love of his neighbor. Two things
the naturally bright and in many respects interesting people of Korea especially need, and which
the present system of education certainly fails to
give them, are a broader intellectual view and a
deepened moral sense.   Their present system of
intellectual and moral training then, needs evidently much to supplement it.   The Chino-Japanese war, in a number of respects, deep-soil
plowed the life and institutions of Korea.   One of
the institutions which early disappeared was the
Koaga, or royal examination, held periodically
through the spring and fall, when the streets used
to be filled with country scholars, all aspirants for
literary degrees. These literary titles were, in the
ante-bellum days, greatly prized, largely no doubt
because the rank thus obtained was believed to
furnish a stepping-stone toward the acquisition of
government office, the *summum bonum* of the Korean scholar.   But with the passing of the *Koaga*
and a change in the methods of government
appointments, it may be questioned whether much
of the incentive to the acquisition of an education
of the time-honored variety has not also passed
away. It may be further queried, if this be true—
that the interest in education is waning throughout the country—What other educational forces are
there at work, whose influence can be counted
upon to stimulate in some measure this flagging

interest in all education; and can they be said to
give promise of supplying the lacking elements
mentioned above, a broadened mental outlook or
a deepened moral sense? The answer is that
there are three classes of schools whose influence
radiates from the capital—government vernacular
schools, government schools for the study of foreign languages, and missionary institutions of
learning, all of which aim to impart nineteenth
century knowledge and, in varying degrees, seek
the moral culture of their students. Let it be
understood that in this chapter we are viewing
conditions that existed in the late spring of 1896,
at which time the author, pencil and note-book
in hand, made a tour of the schools and collected
the data here presented. Referring now to the
first class of government schools mentioned, the
writer's information was largely derived from Mr.
T. H. Yun, the then Acting Minister of Education,
who later became a member of the embassy sent
to represent Korea at the coronation of the "Czar
of all the Russias." It may be remarked in passing that his experience and Christian education in
a foreign land seemed to have peculiarly fitted
Mr. Yun for usefulness in the position he then
held. These schools came largely into being
during the so-called "reform era." The scheme
of education embraces a system of primary schools,
with a normal school for the training of the teachers. The normal school, located in Kyo-tong,
was organized in 1895 with a Japanese instructor

in charge.   Two Korean teachers at the time of my visit were guiding their studies.*

The subjects taught consisted of history (Korean and universal), simple arithmetic, geography, Chinese and Unmun composition, and the Chinese classics. Candidates for admission to the normal school must be able to read and write Chinese and the age limits range between eighteen and twenty-five years.   The aim was to accommodate fifty pupils, fed and lodged at government expense.   It was expected that, after order was restored in the country, with teachers drawn from this normal school, primary schools would be started in each of the provincial capitals of the country.   Already there existed in the city of Seoul five flourishing primary schools.   With the exception of one which numbers about 150, the average number of scholars enrolled in each of the schools is 100.   The monthly wages paid are as follows: for a normal school-teacher, forty yen; for a primary school-teacher, fourteen yen.

Referring now to the second variety of schools for the study respectively of Japanese, French, Russian and English, the Japanese school, located in Kyo-tong, has been in existence since 1890. It is in charge of the genial Mr. I. Nagashima, a graduate of Tokyo University and a teacher of five years' experience in Japan.   Associated with

---

*May 1, 1897, there was a change in management and the Rev. H. B. Hulbert, who will be mentioned later, became the principal of the normal school.

him is Mr. M. Oya, a graduate of the Kanagawa Normal School, and they have one Korean assistant. The students are divided into two classes, and number forty. The average age is nineteen, ranging from sixteen to thirty years. The studies embrace the learning of Japanese, the study of Western branches through the medium of the Japanese, and physical drill. The writer heard one day the advanced class read in concert, in alternation with the teacher, and to judge by the sound the reading was remarkably fluent and accurate.

The French and Russian schools are located in the spacious school property at Pak Tong, southeast of the palace. These schools are among our most recent acquisitions, the Russian school having been opened May 10th and the French school about the first of January, 1896. In charge of the Russian school is Mr. N. Birukoff, late captain of light artillery in the Russian army; and the teacher of the French school is Mr. E. Martel. Both have had experience in private teaching. They have each a Korean assistant. The students in attendance at the Russian school are thirty-six; in the French school thirty-four; the average age in the Russian school is twenty-two, ranging from sixteen to forty; in the French school seventeen, ranging from fifteen to thirty years. The study in these schools is yet largely linguistic, but western branches will be rapidly introduced in the respective languages taught.

Daily physical drill is given the pupils of both schools under the superintendence of members of the Russian legation guard. These schools, although so recently established, are in a flourishing condition, and with a bright class of pupils, and excellent instructors, a highly successful career may be anticipated for them.

English education in Seoul had its origin in Mr. T. E. Hallifax's School for Interpreters, which, from the year 1883, was held for a period of three years in the Foreign Office. The pupils numbered thirty-five and their ages ranged from fifteen to thirty. Very good work was done, as is evidenced by the fact that fifteen former members of the school now hold positions in the various ports. In the spring of 1885 General John Eaton, the well-known commissioner of education, in compliance with a request to the U. S. government from his majesty, received instructions from the government to secure three suitable men, who should repair to Korea to take charge of a government school for the teaching of English. His choice fell upon three students in Union Theological Seminary, New York City, two of whom were about to graduate, Rev. G. W. Gilmore of Princeton, '83, Rev. D. A. Bunker, Oberlin, '83, and Rev. H. B. Hulbert, Dartmouth, '84. The government school was organized September 23, 1886. Each teacher had a Korean interpreter. As soon as practicable Western studies were introduced, which were taught through the medium of

English text-books. In addition to the ordinary elementary studies, the elements of international law and political economy were taught. The pupils enrolled were about one hundred. Two examinations of the school were held before his majesty, at one of which the writer had the honor of being present.

As the result of the work of the school a number of good men were turned out, one of whom is the Minister of Foreign Affairs, another is Secretary of Legation at Tokyo, and a third is assistant Postmaster in the Korean postoffice at Chemulpo. Capable, earnest work was done by the instructors; but in some respects the school did not prosper as it deserved, for his majesty's good intentions were frustrated, after the fashion of those ante-bellum days, by the peculating officials connected with the school, who diverted to the extent of their ability the funds of the institution to their private use, so that, becoming disheartened, first Mr. Gilmore, then Mr. Hulbert, and finally Mr. Bunker resigned and returned to America, the last two metioned, however, coming back later as members of the Methodist Mission. We come now to another stage in the history of the Royal English School. Mr. W. du F. Hutchison was engaged from the fall of 1893 in teaching English upon the island of Kang-wha, in connection with the school for naval cadets. In the late fall of 1894 he was transferred to Seoul to fill the vacancy made by the departure of Mr.

Bunker, in the English school at Pak Dong.   He brought with him a score of his former pupils; four old scholars of the Pak Dong school were added, and the government sent still others, aggregating sixty-four students.   The Royal School continued at Pak Dong till the first of 1895, when the school property was turned temporarily into police barracks, and the school was transferred to its present quarters in the telegraph office in front of the palace, just west of the offices of the Department of Agriculture.   Highly creditable work has been done by the school, as was evidenced by the excellent written examination papers prepared in June of 1896.   The teaching force consists of Mr. Hutchison, Mr. T. E. Hallifax and three Korean assistants.   These three assistant teachers receive each a monthly payment of from twenty to twenty-five yen.   The number of pupils is one hundred and three, with a daily average of ninety-two.   It may be remarked in passing that an indication of the discipline of the school was seen when the writer, on a very rainy day, visited the school and found the entire body of pupils in attendance.   Their average age is nineteen years, ranging in fact from sixteen to twenty-eight years.   The branches taught consist of a study of colloquial English, reading English, English composition, arithmetic, grammar, writing, translation to and from English and Chinese, also the same with Unmun and English, and lessons in general knowledge in the form of practical talks.

Physical training is imparted by a sergeant from the English legation guard, in the form of marching, calisthenics, and a drill with staves, known technically as the "Swedish physical drill." By the time my visit to the Royal School was made, Mr. Yun had been succeeded as Minister of Education by a Mr. Sin, a deeply dyed conservative, who was destined, however, not to remain long in office, and a very decided clash between the minister and the school was in progress over the wearing by the pupils of a neat foreign uniform, consisting of a jacket, trousers and a cap of white duck cloth with red trimmings. Suffice it to say that the scholars won the day. The aim of the school is to turn out men with a good general knowledge, in addition to proficiency in the use of English.

Still another class of schools is deserving of our attention—institutions under missionary auspices. The first to claim our attention is a school which, strictly speaking, does not belong in this class, but on account of other features connected with the plan of which it is a part, it may properly be mentioned here. The latest arrival in the educational field of Korea is the school established April 16, 1896, by representatives of the "Japanese Foreign Educational Society." The contributors to this society are Japanese Christians and non church-members, the majority of which body, however, are members of evangelical churches. The location of the school is on the western edge

of Chin-go-kai, immediately behind the site of
the new Japanese consulate. The teachers are
Messrs. K. Koshima and M. Zingu, both of whom
are graduates of the Doshisha College at Kyoto,
and have been for two years students in the
theological seminary of the same institution. They
have for their assistants two Koreans who speak
Japanese. The students in attendance are fifty-
eight, who are divided into three classes. The
average age is twenty-three, ranging from ten to
thirty-eight years. The curriculum includes a
limited study of the Chinese classics, also Unmun
composition, the learning of Japanese, and the
study of Western learning through the medium of
the Japanese; and further, a weekly lecture is
delivered, through an interpreter, on scientific
and religious subjects. No direct religious teaching forms a part of the course of study on account
of the mixed nature of the society founding the
school. But the teachers are Christians, with a
missionary purpose; and the plan and hope is
that, later, men will be sent to work with them
who shall give their entire time to religious work
and the establishment of churches. That such
an enterprise should be undertaken at all is a striking indication of the fact that Christianity has
become native to the soil of Japan.

The representatives of the "Société des Missions Étrangères," of Paris, have in the city of
Seoul and its immediate vicinity three varieties of
schools, an orphanage, two boys' schools and a

theological seminary.   The orphanage was organized by the French fathers in 1883 in Myeng-
tong, with ten Korean assistants   In 1888 the
oversight of the school was transferred to the
Sisters of the Community of St. Paul of Chartres.
In 1890 the orphanage was moved by the Sisters
to their present commodious quarters, north of
Chin-go-kai, the Japanese settlement.   The
expenses of the institution are chiefly defrayed
by the Society of Ste. Enfance, of Paris.   The
children received are almost entirely orphans
whose parents have had no connection with the
Catholic Church.   Connected with the school are
five French sisters, one Chinese sister, also Korean novices ten, *postulantes* ten, and *aspirants*
nine.   In the school are sixty boys, with ages
ranging from five to thirteen years, eighty-nine
girls of the same ages, thirty-nine small children
from two to five years old and fifty-four infants,
making a total of 242 children.   The older girls
study Unmun, learn the church catechism and
various forms of prayer, and are instructed in
sewing and general housework.   The larger boys
study Unmun, read stories selected from the Bible,
and learn the catechism and various forms of
prayer.   Formerly these boys were taught to
make mats, pouch-strings and cigarettes, but
three years ago the plan was abandoned as unprofit-
able.   The younger children are taught verbally
forms of prayer.   When the girls arrive at an age
of from thirteen to fifteen years they are married

to the children of adherents. Boys thirteen years
old are adopted by members of the church in the
city and country, and learn farming or one of the
trades; or, assuming their own support, become
servants or enter some trade. The object of the
school is to train into good Catholics these unfortunate children, bereaved of a parent's protection.

Referring now to the two boys' schools mentioned above, one of them, opened in 1883, is
located on the northern edge of Chin-go-kai; the
other, opened in 1893, is connected with the
French fathers' place at Yak-hyon, outside the
south gate of the city. Each consists of twenty-
five boys, under a Korean teacher. Their average
age is ten, ranging from five to fifteen years. In
these schools the boys are taught to read and write
Chinese and Unmun, with a limited study of the
Chinese classics. In the Unmun they are taught
the catechism and forms of prayer. The scholars
are all catechumens or church members. The
aim of the schools is to provide a native and religious primary education for the children of the
members of the church. The theological seminary, now located three miles from the city, on the
bluff by the river, at Yong-san, was organized in
1854 or '55 in the village of Chyei-tchou in the
Kang-won province, under the title of "Pai-ron
Hak-tang." In 1866, the year of the great massacre of the French fathers and their disciples, the
school was broken up. In the dark years that
followed, the efforts put forth by aspirants to the

priesthood to secure a priestly education are interesting.   In 1871 one such student, crossing over
from Korea, sought the theological school at Cha-
ling in Lao-tung, Manchuria, where eight years
later he died.   Three other youths, who, for three
years, had been studying with priests in conceal-
ment in Korea, were in 1880 sent across the border
to this school in Cha-ling.   In 1882 they were
removed to Nagasaki, Japan, where their numbers were gradually increased by the arrival of
other students, who came from Korea in groups
of twos and threes.   In 1883 this band of students
was sent to Penang in the Straits Settlements,
where they remained until 1891 or '92, when,
on account of sickness, they returned to Yong-
san, their number being then twenty-four.   In
the meantime in Pu-ung-kol, a small Catholic village near Won-ju, in Kang-won-to, a Latin school
had been opened in 1885.   This was removed to
Yong-san in 1888, where the large brick seminary
building was erected which opened its doors in
1891.   There are at present in charge of the theological seminary, Fathers Rault and Bret; and
under them are one Korean sub-deacon and a
Korean teacher of Chinese.   The present number
of students is twenty-three.   Their average age
is nineteen, ranging from fourteen to thirty-two
years.   The studies of the seminary are grouped in
three consecutive courses, these courses being in
Latin, philosophy and theology; but the students
are divided into four classes.   New students are

admitted to the school every four years, who enter upon the studies of the Latin course. These new students are presently divided into two divisions, the brighter students forming an advanced class with a four-years' course, while the others pursue a course of seven years in the same studies. Graduates from the Latin course take a course of one year in philosophy. Then they study theology for three years or until they can pass the required examinations that are held semi-annually. In the Latin course, in addition to the study of Latin, there are taught arithmetic, geography, history, natural philosophy and music. In the philosophical course there is the study of metaphysics, logic, ethics and theodicy. The studies in the theological course consist of dogmatics, moral theology, study of the Bible, and training in the ritual of the church. Throughout the entire seminary course the Chinese classics are studied daily. The object of the school is to train suitable young men to enter the orders of the priesthood.

The girls' school of the Presbyterian Mission (north) came into being with a group of little girls Mrs. Bunker gathered about her in 1888. Mrs. Gifford, at that time Miss M. E. Hayden, arrived in the late fall of the same year, and at once took them under her care. She was succeeded in 1890 by Miss S. A. Doty, who, with the exception of one year, has remained the superintendent of the school ever since. She was joined in 1892 by Misses E. Strong and V. C. Arbuckle, who, two

years later, left the school; the former on account
of ill-health, and the latter in order to take up
the work of nursing in the government hospital.
The location of the girls' school was formerly in
the foreign settlement, but the fall of 1895 saw
them domiciled in their new home at Yon-mot-kol
("Lotos pond district"), two miles away from the
former site, on the eastern side of the city.
With a plant of buildings far better suited to the
needs of the institution, the outlook for the school
is bright.   A girls' school in Korea is something
more than a school.   It is an evangelistic center
which attracts to it Korean women from the region
round about.   So, connected with the school, is a
chapel where women are daily met for religious
teaching and a dispensary, visited periodically by
Dr. Whiting.   Among   the   girls   themselves
a   Christian   Endeavor   Society   exists.   The
number of pupils consists of twenty-eight boarders and one day scholar.   The average age of the
girls is twelve, ranging from eight to seventeen.
As for the teaching force, Miss Doty is in charge,
with Miss K. C. Wambold, newly arrived, preparing herself to join in the work.   The assistants
are two Korean women.   Then twice a week Miss
Strong drills them in kindergarten work.   Also
twice a week Mrs. Gifford has the older girls in
Old Testament historical studies.   Now a word or
two on the studies taught.   At first the little girls
were set to singing the Chinese characters; but
this was presently given up and now all the

instruction is conveyed through the medium of the Unmun.   In addition to the studies mentioned above, the girls are taught the reading and writing of Unmun, arithmetic, geography and study of various Gospels and religious books printed in the Unmun.   Perhaps the most interesting feature is that the little girls are given a systematic and thorough training in all the work pertaining to a Korean household.   The writer has seen specimens of their needle-work, more especially in the line of Korean embroidery, which were excellently done.   The aims of the school are to first lead them to become Christians—not only so, but active Christians, well grounded in the faith, and with a good mental training, that they may be made self-reliant, ready to cope with the situation in which they find themselves placed, whatever it may be.

Passing now to schools for youth connected with the Presbyterian Mission, the first to be established was the medical school opened by Dr. Allen in the fall of 1885, with a proper amount of appliances, including a skeleton that has been frightening people ever since its arrival in the country.   The school was located at the government hospital.   The medical instruction was imparted through the medium of the English; and assisting in the school were Doctors Heron and Underwood.   On the departure of Dr. Allen to America, in 1887, the nature of the institution was changed to that of a school for the teaching of English, and so continued for the space of two years.

The present "Yasu Kyo Hak-tang" ("Jesus Doctrine School"), located in Chong-tong, the foreign settlement, was instituted by Dr. Underwood in the spring of 1886, in the form of an orphanage, modeled on the plan of those well-known institutions in England. The instruction was in English, Chinese and Unmun. In 1890, when Dr. Underwood returned temporarily to America, the plan of the institution was materially changed under the superintendence of Mr. Moffett. You may or you may not be aware that there are two excellent sides to the question of the advisability of teaching English in mission schools. Without going into the merits of the question, suffice it to say that from that time all the teaching in the school has been through the medium of the Chinese and Unmun. The nature of the school also was changed from an orphanage to a day and boarding school for boys. In 1893 the charge of the school passed into the hands of the present superintendent, Rev. F. S. Miller. The number of the pupils is fifty-five, with a daily average of forty. Eight are fed and clothed by the school, but partially support themselves by manual labor. The average age is thirteen, ranging from nine to seventeen years. The regular teaching force consists of Mr. Miller, with one Korean teacher and two assistants. On various days in the week supplementary teaching is supplied by Mrs. Miller, Mr. Bell and Dr. Vinton. Let us glance at the course of study. There are

the reading and writing of the Chinese and
Unmun. There is a limited study of the Chinese
classics, followed by a study of the Bible and
Christian books in the Chinese. In Unmun a
number of Christian books are studied, physical
and political geography, arithmetic, physiology,
history of the Christian Church, and training in
singing. Drill in marching is given by a member of the U. S. legation guard. Some of the
lads who are fed and clothed contribute to their
support by sawing lumber; others assist in the
government hospital and the dispensaries; still
others do janitor work. It is worthy of mention
that the lads at the hospital are being given a
medical training by Dr. Avison. The aim of the
school is to furnish a strongly Christian general
education. Some of the boys are very aggressive
little Christian workers, selling Christian books to
men on the streets and telling them about Jesus.
I noticed one day a group of men standing beside
the street listening quietly and with evident
respect. The center of the group was a school
boy with a roll of books under his arm, telling
them in his imperfect way what it was to become
a Christian. The plan is to make the school in
Seoul supplement Christian primary schools in
the country and out-stations, developing it into
a normal and high school,* to which the gradu-

* At the annual meeting of 1897, it was decided to temporarily close the Presbyterian boys' school and release Mr.
Miller to do evangelistic work in the Whang-hai province,
where the pressure is so great.

ates of the primary schools may be sent; it should
also be mentioned that at the house of Rev. S.
F. Moore, of the Presbyterian Mission, is a primary Christian school where some twenty boys are
under instruction.

The Presbyterian Mission has also in mid-winter
a month's or six weeks' training class for religious workers, chiefly from the country.

Let us now turn to the M. E. school known by
the poetical name given it by his majesty—the
"Ewa Hak-tang" or "Pear-flower School." This
school for girls was organized in June, 1886, by
Mrs. M. F. Scranton, and was moved into its
commodious quarters on the hill in the foreign
settlement in November of the same year.   Mrs.
Scranton tells of the prejudice she had to over-
come in those early days; for people were afraid
to put their children into the school, because they
thought they would never see them again. When
Mrs. Scranton took her furlough, in 1891, the
school passed under the care of Miss L. C. Roth-
weiler, who had been with her since 1887.   Later
arrivals at the school were Mrs. G. H. Jones (née
Miss Bengel) in 1891, Misses J. O. Paine and L.
E. Frey, and Mrs. Dr. Follwell (formerly Miss
M. W. Harris), in 1893. The teaching force consists of Miss Paine, who has been in charge since
1893, and associated with her, Miss Frey.   The
Korean assistants are one woman and three pupil
teachers.   Certain days in the week also Mrs.
Bunker teaches them fine sewing and embroidery,

and Mrs. Hulbert trains them in vocal music. The pupils number forty-seven boarders and three day-scholars. The average age is twelve years, with ages ranging between eight and seventeen years. English and Unmun are the media through which knowledge is imparted. Elementary Western branches are taught in English; certain Western studies and religious literature are studied in Unmun. English is optional and is taught to perhaps one third of the girls. The domestic economy of the school is interesting. In addition to the training in sewing and embroidery, native, and foreign, mentioned above, the clothes of all are made and cared for by the older girls. Then the school is divided into eight groups according to their rooms, each under a leader and sub-leader, who turn-about, two weeks at a time, clean rooms and schoolrooms and assist in the culinary department. The leader in each case is made responsible for all that goes on in the room. The capacity of the school building was already too small. In the fall it was planned to open a Chinese department; and instrumental music would be taught in the future to a few. The aim of the school is to give a thorough Christian education and to make them better Korean women.

Let us turn now to another institution of the Methodist Mission, the "Pai Chai College," so named by his majesty in 1887, the meaning of the title being "Hall for the rearing of useful men." With the exception of one year, Rev. Mr. Appenzeller has been in charge from the time of its institution in 1886. There have been on the teaching force at various times in the past Revs. G. H. Jones, F. Ohlinger, and W. A. Noble. A fine brick building was erected in 1887, in the foreign settlement, at a cost of $4,000. In March, 1895, the Educational Department of the Korean Government expressed the desire to place a number of pupils in the institution; and an agreement was entered into whereby pupils up to a limit of 200 could be sent to the school by the government. It was stipulated that not only their tuition, but also the salaries of certain tutors, in the ratio of one tutor to every fifty pupils sent, should be paid from the national treasury. The present teaching force consists of Mr. Appenzeller as principal; in charge of academic department Mr. Bunker; and of Korean assistants three tutors in English, and three in Chinese. Dr. Philip Jaisohn also delivers lectures to the school once a week. The institution is divided as follows: into a Chinese, an English, and a theological department. As to the number of students, there are 106 in the English and 60 in the Chinese department. In the theological department, under the charge of Mr. Appenzeller, there were six students in attendance at the last session. The average age of the pupils in the Chinese department is twelve years; in the English department, eighteen years. The studies taught in the English department are reading, grammar, composition, spelling, history, arithmetic, and the elements of chemistry and natural philosophy. In the Chinese department there are taught the Chinese classics *ad infinitum*, Sheffield's Universal History, also in the Unmun certain religious works. The attendance at chapel is compulsory. An Epworth League exists in the school. The pupils are drilled by a member of the American legation guard and have come out in a neat school uniform of white duck cloth, trimmed with red and blue stripes. The aim to establish an industrial department has been kept in mind from the outset. Some time since the attempt was made to open a department for the manufacture of brush pens and straw sandals. The superintendent once explained to the writer the result of the experiment. He said that he had remarked that men who bought the pens his scholars made never came back for any more. With Oriental politeness they explained to him that the pens were excellent, only they would not write. He thought it must have been something the same way with the shoes. At all events it was not long before his shoe and pen factory went into bankruptcy. However, later efforts were more successful. It is said that the idea of founding the "Tri-lingual Press" by the M. E. Mission, originated largely from the desire to devise employment for students who were being gratuitously fed. Impecunious students now earn their living in a variety of ways. Students are em-

ployed as personal teachers, to do scribal work and
to care for the rooms. The "Korean Repository"
is printed, with one exception, entirely by boys
from the school. Foreign binding has been done
by students; and as for Korean binding, in the
bindery in the basement of the school, established
the previous fall, twenty boys find employment.
As evidence of their efficiency it may be
stated that from December to June, 1896, over
50,000 volumes have been bound by them. The
aim of the institution is education *per se*—a
liberal education.

Two Christian primary schools for boys are
also conducted by the M. E. Mission, one at San-
tong and one immediately inside the East Gate.

A writer in the "Korean Repository" has
expressed the opinion that of all the things Korea
greatly needs at the present moment, a true education of heart and mind is what she needs the
most; and in the foregoing pages some idea may
have been formed of the forces which, combined,
have been seeking to supply that need.

CHAPTER XIV

It is a widely-recognized principle among the missionary workers in foreign lands, and among all the mission board secretaries, that the ideal toward which, so far and so fast as it is practicable they shall aim to conduct their work, is a condition of affairs in which the native church becomes rooted in the soil of the local country. One phase which has in recent years received much attention has been the effort to make the native churches self-supporting in their finances. Two things have rendered this difficult. One is the fact that in some countries the work has been started with the other policy, the churches being built and the salaries of the native ministers being paid, wholly or in large part, with foreign funds; and, having begun on this plan, the effort to shift the financial burden to native shoulders has been resisted by the native congregations. But a still more serious difficulty has been the great comparative and actual poverty of the church members, few of whom come from the classes that possess means.

In Korea, the youngest of mission countries, we are making an honest attempt in the direction of self-support. The ministers' pay has not become a practical question, because as yet we have ordained none. In the matter of church building, however, we are able to make a report of progress. Allow me to speak of certain church-building operations that came under my own observation; and to properly tell the story I shall need to mention briefly some of the earlier history of the church. The first Presbyterian Church in Seoul was organized by Rev. Dr. Underwood, and from the time of his temporary return to America, on account of the health of Mrs. Underwood, the superintendence of the church work fell to various others of us clerical men in conjunction with Mr. Saw, the evangelist. The meetings of the church were held in an "L" shaped building upon Dr. Underwood's compound in the foreign settlement. In those early days the regular church attendance was not large, and probably a majority of those present were, those attached to us in some manner—as teachers, servants, or school children. The first efforts to raise money among the church attendants came from themselves, when, following the Korean custom, they organized among themselves an association for the loaning of money, with the view to mutual help at the times of weddings or funerals, which are so costly for Koreans. As we thought such an organization was best conducted as a private enterprise, we took no ecclesiastical notice of it. Later we organized a church collections committee, composed of two Koreans and one foreigner. As they slipped off their shoes outside and rattled the Korean cash, bulky in amount and small in value, into the soap box by the door, they slightly disturbed the meeting, but in the interest of education in church-giving we were quite willing to be disturbed. As the years passed by our church attendance grew, and in 1895 Mrs. Gifford, who was at that time in charge of the work among the women of the church, complained that the space on the women's side of the curtain would no longer hold the female congregation, and she urged that a new church be built. The members of the Northern and Southern Presbyterian missions took up the plan, and a committee consisting of Dr. Underwood and Mrs. Gifford was appointed to secure pledges and build the church with foreign funds, as it hardly seemed possible that much financial help could be expected from our Korean brethren. Ground had been bought not far from the foreign settlement, on a wide street just inside the West Gate of the city, and the buildings on it had been removed, when news came to us that the Korean Christians at Chang-yen, a country district perhaps one hundred miles northwest of Seoul, had built a church that had cost them forty yen and fully that amount of labor, under the inspiration of the lamented Rev. W. J. McKenzie, a strong believer in native self-support, then living in their midst. Courage was therefore given us to try what a couple of the Southern brethren had previously advocated—to put the burden of the erection of the church upon the shoulders of the Korean Christians. I happened at that time to be the pastor of the Chong Dong church, and I conducted a mid-week prayer-meeting for men every Wednesday noon. On one particular Wednesday it was arranged that at the close of the meeting a business meeting of the church should be held. Dr. Underwood was called down to the *sarang*, and I, partly as pastor and partly representing Mrs. Gifford, joined with him in conducting the meeting. I can see the picture now. The sliding doors which divided the *sarang* into sections had been taken out. We sat at one end. The Korean men formed a long double line, as they sat cross-legged along the sides of the room. What interesting work they made in following our parliamentary rules in the conduct of the meeting! The plan that they should undertake the erection of the church building seemed to impress them favorably. They cheerfully elected, with the few parliamentary stumbles above mentioned, a Korean committee, consisting of Deacons Hong and Ye, who were to act jointly with the committee of foreigners. Dr. Underwood and I, thinking that we had accomplished all that could be done for some time, were about to close the meeting, when Deacon Ye deliberately made the remark that the building operations had better begin right away. My own mind at once reverted to the great Catholic cathedral, over in the city, since completed, whose unfinished brick walls had stretched towards the sky ever since my arrival in the country, and I pictured a similar fate for the building whose construction it was proposed to begin with only a few cash in the treasury. Dr. Underwood and one Korean voiced our sentiment when they urged that the money first be raised. But no, Mr. Ye thought they had better begin at once, and what was more remarkable, the rest of the men in the room quite agreed with him. And so it was voted.

Dr. Underwood was called to the country about that time; so the burden of seeking to carry through the plan came upon the Korean committee and myself. Deacon Hong, also my helper, being gifted with mechanical ability, was put in charge of the construction; while Deacon Ye and I undertook to raise subscriptions. We canvassed every member of the church, then the members of the two or three little churches that had recently swarmed into other parts of the city, then a couple of Christian officials whom we knew. The same was done among the women of the church. But to carry the plan through it was absolutely necessary that the Korean men in the church should contribute work. But this was hard for many of them, as they considered themselves to belong to the gentleman class, and thought they would lower themselves should they labor with their hands. So, by way of example,

I put on my old clothes and worked three after-
noons at various forms of coolie work.   One day
it was shoveling dirt in grading the church site.
A Korean shovel, you know, consists of an iron-
shod wooden spade, with a handle six feet long.
Into its wooden sides are bored holes, and two
long straw ropes are inserted.   Then three or
more men take hold of the two ropes and the
shovel handle, and while the man at the handle
guides the operations, they vigorously heave the
dirt.   Another day the work was the braiding of
straw ropes.   The third day we pounded broken
tiles and stones into the holes into which the
foundation stones to support the wooden pillars
were to be inserted.   This was done with a
boulder to which were attached a dozen straw
ropes.   Men and boys took hold of the ropes and
straightened out as in tossing with a blanket; at a
signal they relaxed, and the stone fell like a trip-
hammer.   Koreans turn this work into a frolic,
by heaving the stone in time to the chanting of a
chorus that is sung responsively to the solo singing, usually improvised, of one of their number.
The men of the church took hold of the work in a
very gratifying manner, as did the small boys in
the school, who, after school hours, helped in all
ways possible to them—for instance, scouring the
streets of the city for broken tiles and stones.
When skilled labor was required, Mr. Hong called
in a carpenter and the men worked under his
instructions.   I believe it became necessary to

pass around the subscription paper a second time.

A very curious thing occurred. One morning early a visitor called upon me. He proved to be a tall, elderly man, who occasionally attended our meetings. His errand was to tell me that a friend of his, living in the country, had heard from him about the building of the church, and wished to make a contribution. An hour later Mr. Hong came in. He told me that timbers for the frame work of the church were coming that day, and that they needed just twenty yen to complete payment for them. I then told him of the man who was coming at 10 o'clock that morning to contribute just exactly that amount, twenty yen, to the work. Promptly at the hour named Mr. Shin, a perfect stranger to us all, put in his appearance. Two or three of the Korean brethren and myself met him in a room adjoining the church site. Twenty silver yen were taken from a roll and deposited in our midst on the floor. He had brought along also a couple of packages of tobacco as a present to the committee in charge of the work; but they decided, I believe, to sell it and turn the proceeds into the building fund. We talked with him a long time, instructing him in the way of salvation, and before we parted he knelt and prayed for the forgiveness of his sins. I gave him some Christian books, and he went to his home in the country. I have since seen him once or twice, and I could never discover that there had been any ulterior motive in what he did. I could never explain this singular event in any other way than that God had, in answer to prayer, put it into this stranger's heart to bring us just the amount that was needed. In this connection let me remark that many of us missionaries have learned to count upon prayer as just as practical a factor in our work as the preparation of our financial estimates.

Mrs. Gifford and I, being transferred to the eastern side of the city to look after religious work in the neighborhood of the girls' school, Dr. Underwood resumed the pastorate of the Chong Dong church; and the latter half of the church building operations was done under his superintendence, in co-operation with the Korean committee. With the coming of the rainy season appeared the scourge of Asiatic cholera; and building operations being suspended on account of the rains, Dr. Underwood took the entire force of Christian men over to help him, Mrs. Underwood and Dr. Wells in their improvised cholera hospital, at the "Shelter," outside the city. It was a time when a majority of the missionaries in Seoul devoted themselves to the care of the sick and the dying. As the result of their untiring exertions and the skillful use of salol, the Doctors Underwood and Wells saved 66 percent. of the patients in their hospital. The Korean Christians, at the end of their noble and perilous service, were generously remembered by the government; and a large part of what was given them they turned into the church-building fund. But still there was not enough money. Then those church members who were employed by missionaries as teachers, in addition to all they had previously given secured from their employers an advance of one month's wages, which they were to repay in installments, and this they turned into the treasury. I know of some of the extra efforts and the sacrifices that Korean Christians made in order to raise this building fund. Women did sewing in order to raise money. One Christian, outside of working hours, painted a sign-board for a chapel, and pawned his spectacles. One woman, working as a servant in a foreign family at the rate of four yen, or two of our dollars, a month, for several months contributed fully a fifth of her wages. Her employer expostulated with her for giving so much; but the woman said that it was a pleasure for her to give all that she could for the work. The church, when built, was a rectangular, tiled-roof building, in thorough Korean style, with a row of pillars and a partition running up through the middle of the church as far as the pulpit platform, to separate the men and the women. It holds between two and three hundred people. Here are held the preaching services, Sabbath School and mid-week prayer meeting. The contributions of the Korean Christians amounted to fully five hundred yen, and, since the yen is worth about fifty cents of our

money, equal approximately to $250. Probably
an equal value in labor was freely given. This
is better understood when you remember that $4
of our money per month is a high average for
the wages earned by the men of the church.
The total contributions of this church for the
year 1897 have amounted to $203.55 (yen). And
that they are as earnest on the spiritual side of
the work as they are in looking after its material
interests is seen in the fact that they have themselves been teaching eighteen catechumen classes
in the city and suburbs, and have been conducting regular, active work in eight or more villages within a radius of thirty miles from
Seoul. This surely is a good record for one
church.

Other circles of believers have done well also.
The Chang-yen church, referred to above, have
since doubled the size of their church building.
In the regions about Pyeng-yang twenty-three
small churches have been built or adapted from
existing buildings; also in the southern part of
the Whang Hai province and in the vicinity of
Seoul eleven more have been prepared, all
with money and work contributed by the Koreans. Perhaps a dozen Christian primary schools
are supported in part from native funds; and the
Koreans are paying the salaries of certain of their
number, who go about the country adjacent to
Pyeng-yang and Seoul as colporteurs. The record of the Methodist brethren is also good; for

their Korean Christians in Seoul also raised seven hundred yen, which they combined with foreign funds in the erection of a large brick church, with a foreign exterior, located in the middle of the foreign settlement. But what has touched me most, revealing as it does in the Korean believers the depth of that Christ-like compassion for need and suffering outside of its own circle, and that looks for no advantage in return—the same motive which impels you, the givers to foreign missions, to send the beneficent Gospel to them, and a motive for which you will look in vain in a purely heathen community—was their conduct at the time of the late famine in India. The "Repository" and "Independent" make mention of it. The "Christian News," published in Seoul, at the close of a graphic account of the terrible famine, intimated the willingness of the editor to forward any contributions sent to him. The response from the Korean Christians was hearty and immediate. The Presbyterian churches of Seoul raised some sixty odd yen. The Methodists and Presbyterians of Pyeng-yang sent fully as much more. The Christians of Chang-yen also took up a collection, to which the "Repository" for May alluded as follows: "Some of the women, not having ready cash with them, took the rings off their fingers, as no less than eight solid silver rings were among the contributions sent to Seoul. These rings were sold and netted twenty-seven yen and fifty sen—making a total of over eighty-four yen contributed by this congregation to the starving ones in India."

In the face of facts like the foregoing, I suppose the critics of missions will continue to shake their heads and moan, "Foreign missions are a failure. The native converts are all 'rice Christians.'"

CHAPTER XV

The name of the city of Pyeng-yang, under half a dozen forms of spelling, is now world-famous as the scene of one of the most decisive battles in the recent Chino-Japanese war. It is by far the most important city in the north of Korea, located perhaps 180 miles to the north of Seoul, upon the Tatong River, and said to have had in the days before the war a population of 100,000 people. Its history carries us back to the times of Samuel the judge, when the Chinese statesman Keja made the site of the city of Pyeng-yang his home, and became the founder of Korean civilization. One gets a curious composite impression of ancient and modern history in visiting the grave of Keja, situated just north of the city. Upon the top of a knoll the semi-globular grave, with a low, tiled stone wall half surrounding it, and stone images and a sacrificial slab in front of the mound, remind one of a far antiquity; while the wooden shrine below the knoll, with its walls scarred and perforated in every direction by the bullets of the battle which raged over the site, is very much in evidence of the recent past. During the making of the nation the capital of the country had a wandering life, the most ancient of whose sites, however, was the city of Pyeng-yang. In later days and until the present, the city has been the provincial capital of Pyeng An Do, the most northwestern of the eight provinces into which the country, until recently, has been divided. Again, the city is by far the most important commercial center in the north of Korea. The people are handsome, spirited, energetic, with much force and strength of character, which makes them a power either for good or evil. Indeed, in the past, Pyeng-yang had the reputation for being the wickedest city in the country; one evidence of which was the fact that the city was famed the whole country over for the number of its fair but frail dancing-girls, whose numbers, it is said, have not infrequently been recruited from the more important and influential families of the city. How cruelly the poor city has been punished, however, is evidenced by the great swaths of vacant-house sites here and there visible within the ancient walls, where the homes of the people were razed to the ground by the war. *Yangbans*, or the aristocratic-leisure class, are rare in the city and region. Roman Catholicism has made nothing like the impression in this region that it has in the southern provinces.

There are a number of view points from which it would be interesting to consider quite at length the city of Pyeng-yang; but sufficient, I think,

has been mentioned to indicate the importance of
the city as a strategic point from which to do
religious work. As a rather wonderful religious
movement has sprung up in this northern section
of the country, it will be well to confine our
attention to the opening of missionary work in
Pyeng-yang and its vicinity.

In the early days of the Presbyterian Mission
(North), Dr. Underwood, on one or two occasions,
accompanied by Mr. Appenzeller of the Methodist Mission, made six different visits to the city,
while on his way to and from Eui-Ju, in the
northwestern corner of the country, where he
had work started. On each of these occasions
he spent some time in preaching and selling
Christian books; and at one time he had a couple
of colporteurs located in Pyeng-yang. I may
further mention that in those days Mr. Appenzeller also had a helper living in the city. Upon
the departure of Dr. Underwood to America, in
the spring of 1891, the work in the north fell to
the portion of Rev. S. A. Moffett. For a couple
of years Mr. Moffett made spring and fall trips
to Eui-Ju, spending some time on each occasion
in Pyeng-yang. By 1892 the Presbyterian Mission had reached the conclusion that Pyeng-yang,
in preference to Eui-Ju, was the center where
eventually they hoped to open their station for the
work in the north; and accordingly in the summer of that year Mr. Moffett located his helper,
Mr. Ham Sok Chin, there to do preliminary

work. Mr. Moffett's policy was to win his way
in gradually.

In February, 1893, property was secured for
Mr. Han, with rooms that could be occupied
upon their visits by Mr. Moffett and Rev. Graham
Lee, who had joined him as a colleague in this
northern work. The Methodist Mission, in the
person of W. J. Hall, M.D., also bought buildings at the same time. While the people of the
city showed a friendly disposition, the city magistrate and his underlings disliked the presence of
foreigners, and consequently stirred up trouble.
Messrs. Moffett and Lee thought it wise to give
way before the storm, returned the property
bought for their helper outside the city, and
quietly withdrew. But it was not long before
their helper, Mr. Han, had again bought property, this time inside the East Gate, near the
present site of the Pyeng-yang church, where, in
the fall of the same year, Mr. Moffett quietly
returned to spend the winter, this time being
quite unmolested by the officials of the city.

The winter was spent by Mr. Moffett and his
helper in daily work, which could hardly be called
preaching so much as familiar conversation with
individuals or groups of men wherever they met
them, whether in Mr. Moffett's room, where most
of the work was done, or upon the streets in and
around the city. And the especial themes to
which the conversation was ever brought around
were what the Bible has to say on sin and the

personal need of salvation through Christ. And
it is worthy of note, as one explanation of the
wide spread of Christian work throughout that
northern region, from Pyeng-yang as a center,
that of those who became Christians, many,
whether from precept or example, quickly adopted
the spirit and methods of Mr. Moffett and his
helper in the constant, aggressive "hand-picking"
of souls. Let it be observed that the Holy Spirit
ever continues to bless the faithful, persistent,
personal presentation of the teachings of the Bible
upon these great themes of sin and salvation
through the blood of Christ. There was also a
wide sale and distribution of Scriptures and other
Christian books. This time, in short, was a
period of widespread seed-sowing. Nor was this
all. Mr. Moffett now commenced the systematic
and careful instruction of a group of "catechumens," or applicants for baptism, that began to
gather about them as the result of their evangelistic work. In January, 1894, Mr. Moffett had
the joy of receiving into the church by baptism
seven men, and at the same time formally enroll-
ing as catechumens two others, one of whom, a
Mr. Han, from Anak, in Whang Hai Do, the
next province to the south, I shall have occasion
to mention again in referring to the spread of
the work into the northern part of that province.
These men began at once to tell others what
they had learned of the Gospel truth. The last
of April Mr. Moffett returned to Seoul.

About the 7th of May, 1894, Dr. Hall, of the Methodist Mission, with his wife, his little boy and his household goods, arrived in Pyeng-yang, and moved into the house he had previously purchased. The second night after their arrival began the persecution ever memorable in the history of the work in Pyeng-yang. Seven of the native Christians were holding their regular prayer-meeting in the evening in the room of Mr. Moffett's helper, Mr. Han, when into their midst strode a number of official servants of the magistracy and proceeded to beat them, one of the servants using a ragged piece of cord-wood. They then produced the red cords used for the tying of criminals, and pinioned their arms behind their backs. They stated that the order had come from the king to kill them all for being Christians. Then they started with the party for the city prison, taking with them from the house next door the man who had sold to Mr. Han the house then occupied by him. On the way all were released with the exception of Mr. Han and the former owner of the house, whom they threw into prison.

The same night some one brought word to Dr. Hall that about one o'clock A. M. someone had knocked on the window of his helper, Mr. Kim Chang Sikie, saying that the Doctor had called him. Mr. Kim promptly opened the door, when he was seized, beaten and carried off to prison. The owner of the house bought by Dr. Hall was also seized and imprisoned the same night, and the following forenoon one of the Methodist Christians was also arrested.   Early that morning Dr. Hall went to see the governor, but was told that he was sleeping.   Going to the prison, he found the men with their feet stretched apart and fastened in stocks, in such a manner as to cause them intense pain.   The doctor telegraphed the situation to Seoul.   During the day the prisoners were beaten and money or promissory notes to considerable amounts were extorted from them by the brutal jailers.   A paper came from the officials ordering Dr. Hall out of his house. Later in the day the doctor again sought an interview with the governor; but he refused to see him or grant him any protection.   In the course of the afternoon came telegrams stating that the English and American legations (Dr. Hall was a British subject) would require the Foreign Office to order the release of the men and the granting of protection to Dr. Hall and his family.   Then a runner from the magistracy appeared, demanding the paper brought by him in the morning from the officials ordering Dr. Hall out of his house.   They saw they had gone too far in assuming jurisdiction over a foreigner. The Doctor refused to give it.   The runner stamped about in a rage, and finally seized Dr. Hall's servant by the top-knot, beat him, kicked him, and ordered him taken to prison.   The Doctor then let him have the paper, and the man went away satisfied.

Night settled down over that harassed missionary home and the group of tortured, bleeding Christians in the filthy prison, and what earnest prayers must have risen to God that night for deliverance. In the course of the evening crash came a great stone through the paper window of Mrs. Hall's room. But we are told that God so put his peace into those missionary hearts that they had refreshing sleep. In the morning the water-carriers were forbidden to bring water to Dr. Hall's house. A lying report came to them through an official servant that a telegram had come from Seoul stating that the American and English ministers had seen the king, and as the result of the interview, among other things, the order had been sent to the governor to behead all the Christians. Dr. Hall, on visiting the prison, found that this much was true—the prisoners had been removed to the death cell, where criminals soon to be executed are confined. All day they were threatened, beaten and tortured in the stocks. They tried to make Kim, Han and the other Christians renounce their Christianity; but with the faith of the martyrs they steadily refused. Then to Dr. Hall came the rumor that the governor, who, on account of his being a member of the powerful Min family, to which the queen belonged, did not fear punishment, was about to telegraph to the capital that these men were all Tong Haks, or members of the rebel party then rising throughout the country.

In Seoul all this news, as it was telegraphed,
was very disquieting to the missionary community; and at five o'clock that afternoon a
special prayer-meeting of Methodist and Presbyterian missionaries met at the house of the Rev.
Dr. Underwood.   In the meantime energetic
action was being taken by the legations.   The
British Consul-General, Mr. C. T. Gardiner, now
deceased, a diplomat of thirty years' experience
in China, strongly backed by the former able
American minister, Mr. J. M. B. Sill, brought
heavy and repeated pressure to bear upon
the Foreign Office, demanding the immediate
release of the employes and Christians, and
the missionaries had barely gotten home to
their suppers from that prayer-meeting when the
glad news came over the wires that the prisoners
had been released.   The next morning at daybreak Mr. Moffett and Mr. McKenzie, with chairs
and extra coolies, started for Pyeng-yang, to
travel night and day.   But to take up the thread
of the story in Pyeng-yang.   The night previous,
while the men were still in prison, word came
summoning them before the acting-magistrate of
the city.   Apparently it meant that they were
to be executed.   They were brought before him
and made to kneel in his presence.   He ordered
them to renounce their connection with the foreigners, and to revile the name of God.   The two
house owners, who made no pretensions to Christianity, gladly complied· and one Christian, who

had not known the truth long, abjured his faith under the terrible ordeal. But the two Christian helpers, with the faith of a Paul and a Stephen, refused to do so. Instead of being led without the city to their execution, however, after being beaten they were released. As they started to go an official servant, who had been one of the prime movers in the persecution, set up the cry, "They are all Christians, and no matter if they are killed." Thereupon the whole pack of yamen-runners started after them with stones. Two of the Christians escaped down side streets and were not pursued; but Mr. Kim, Dr. Hall's helper, was stoned all the way home, and staggering into the presence of Dr. Hall, sank to the floor nearly lifeless. Mention should be made here of a school-teacher by the name of Ye, who was at that time living in a village ten miles out from the city. He was a Christian and a friend of Mr. Han, the helper. While the persecution was at its height word came to him of what was transpiring in Pyeng-yang, and he immediately declared his intention of going into the city. His friends protested that should he do so he was liable to be killed. "I cannot help it," was his reply. "Mr. Han is my friend, and I am going in to help him. If Mr. Han dies and the need should exist, I will die with him." But by the time he reached the city the prisoners had been released. In Soon-an, some eighteen miles north of the city, there previously had been a class of twenty inquirers. When news of the troubles in progress reached there, all but three men renounced what little faith they had, and these three hurried into the city to learn the truth regarding the disquieting rumors. As these men afterward did a notable work, mention will be made of them further on.

After the release of the prisoners things became quiet. Messrs. Moffett and McKenzie presently appeared upon the scene and entered upon an investigation of the affair. The authorities were temporarily cowed. Dr. Scranton, of the Methodist Mission, arrived later, and Dr. Hall and family, under the instructions of the British Consul-General, withdrew with him to Seoul. Mr. McKenzie also took his departure. Few people outside of the Christians were coming to see Mr. Moffett and his helper.

It was drawing into the heat of June and the yamen-runners were still muttering their threats, when, partly to get a change from the stifling city, partly to look after country work, and partly to see what would be done by the authorities in his absence, Mr. Moffett paid a visit of a week to Anak, in the next province south, where he stayed holding meetings at the house of Mr. Han, mentioned above as a promising catechumen. After his return the people about the magistracy, finding that no further notice had been taken in Seoul of their maltreatment of people in the employ of the foreigners, became emboldened, and threat-

ened openly to kill all the Christians in Pyeng-
yang as soon as Mr. Moffett left, and sometimes
going so far as to threaten the life of Mr. Moffett
himself.

About this time came the opening of the
Chino-Japanese war. The news of the occupation
of the capital and the taking of the palace by
Japanese troops created a perfect panic among
the citizens of Pyeng-yang. The Christians alone
were calm and went boldly about the city urging
men to put their trust in God. People kept coming to Mr. Moffett for the news. Women
thronged the quarters of helper Han's family as a
refuge from their fears. It was so quiet and
peaceful there, they said, while outside all was
wailing and confusion. This peaceful frame of
mind of the Christians made a considerable
impression upon the people of Pyeng-yang. It
was now becoming really dangerous for Mr.
Moffett to be away from the capital; but so long
as the threat of death hung over the Christians,
he felt it wrong to leave them. The American
minister now brought such pressure to bear upon
the Foreign Office that the authorities in Pyeng-
yang were compelled to refund all the money
that had been extorted from the prisoners and
all the expenditures necessitated in telegraphing
and in special trips to and from the capital,
amounting to 500 yen (about $250), which
amount was paid by Governor Min; and a form
of punishment was inflicted upon the three men

most guilty, or their substitutes. This broke the back of the opposition, and no more threats were heard. News of this vindication of the rights of the missionary and his employes spread all over the country, and, if the expression may be allowed, stock in his religion showed an upward tendency.

Soon after this the Chinese army poured into Pyeng-yang. The position of Mr. Moffett had become precarious. Although he did not know it, only a short time previous Rev. James Wylie, a Scotch Presbyterian missionary, had been murdered in Manchuria by these same troops. He remained close in his room. His servant brought in word that Japanese heads were impaled above the city gates, and all with their hair cut, even to Korean Buddhist priests, were being beheaded on suspicion of being spies. Presently the Korean Christians held a prayer-meeting, and at its close adjourned in a body to urge Mr. Moffett to leave the city, as his presence there was now no longer necessary to their safety. That night he called in the Chinese telegraph operator, who knew him, and through his mediation procured an interview with the Chinese general, as the result of which the general gave orders to put up a notice granting protection to the "Christian chapel," and detailed a squad of soldiers who escorted him on his way to the capital and incidentally seized a city farther south, from which point the party proceeded unattended.

Mr. Moffett's first contact with the Japanese lines nearly proved disastrous. His party was crossing a stone bridge in the dusk of the evening, when suddenly out of a neighboring house rushed four Japanese soldiers, who in an instant of time, with a click, click, click, click, brought to bear their guns upon the party. Needless to say, the company stopped short, in danger of being shot for Chinese scouts. The faces of the guard wore a look of astonishment, over the barrels of their guns, as the tall form of Mr. Moffett, crowned by a tall, white, pith hat, loomed up out of the chair in which he had been riding. A parley was held. Their officer was called, and then his interpreter, who happily proved a Japanese druggist from Pyeng-yang, who knew Mr. Moffett. As the result of his mediation a pass was procured which enabled the party to proceed through the lines in safety to Seoul.

His remaining thus with the Christians in Pyeng-yang until the last moment, while personally dangerous to himself, was no doubt in the end a help to the work, inasmuch as it gave Mr. Moffett a powerful hold upon the affections of those for whom he had ventured so much. From the time of the occupation of Pyeng-yang by the Chinese troops a large portion of its citizens fled to the country, among others the families of Christians. These few Christians, in preparing their loads to go by boat, or making up the packs they were to sling upon their backs, invariably put in a parcel of Christian books. Then, in the villages to which they went, they followed the method they had seen pursued in Pyeng-yang, and preached the Gospel to every man they met, with the result that in those villages a number of people were converted, and still more became inquirers. Nor was this all. The three men mentioned above as inquirers in Soon-an, eighteen miles north from the city, went out preaching the truth in the villages all around their home; and a Mr. Ye, of Pyeng-yang, who died subsequently of cholera, having taken refuge, with his family, from the alarms of war with Mr. Han, of Anak, in the Whang Hai province, seventy miles from the city, he, in company with Mr. Han, went all through the region round about proclaiming the message of the Gospel. From the work done at this time in these two regions to the north and south of Pyeng-yang began the movements which have added so many believers and inquirers in the villages of those respective districts.

Fifteen days after the battle, Messrs. Hall, Lee, and Moffett returned to Pyeng-yang. A pitiful sight met their eyes. Large portions of the city had been laid waste; on the plains round about and here and there through the city were strewn the dead bodies of Chinese soldiers and horses. Mr. Moffett's quarters they found had been looted by Japanese, while Dr. Hall's property and goods were intact, having been protected first by the Chinese and latterly by a Christian Japanese doctor, whom they found in possession. The Japanese troops still occupied the city. The news of the arrival of the missionaries spread through the surrounding country in an incredibly short space of time, and large numbers of men with nothing but a little bundle slung over their backs came flocking into the city, invariably paying first a visit to the missionaries and inquiring, "Is it safe?" and "What is the news?" before returning to their ruined homes. For some time thereafter the movements of the missionaries were watched with breathless interest, and the day they returned to Seoul a large number of men packed up their little bundles and left the city, too, so timorous were they and such confidence did they place in the judgment of the foreigner. The missionaries were astonished at the heartiness of the welcome they received upon this visit from Koreans of every class. Even men who had before opposed them now showed a friendly spirit. Previously, the attitude of mind of the people of the city had been rather distant and suspicious; but now, in the light of the sufferings they had experienced during the war, their eyes were opened to recognize the disinterestedness of the missionaries. Universally they seemed to have come to believe that they were the friends of the people, persons in whom they could put their trust, and from that day to this the missionaries

have experienced nothing but the utmost cordi-
ality in Pyeng-yang upon the part of the Koreans.
The change of attitude was especially noticeable
in the inquirers who from this time kept coming
to them in ever-increasing numbers.   It is, perhaps, needless to say that the fullest advantage of
their opportunities was taken by both the missionaries and the Christians in pressing home the
truths of the Gospel.   During their visit in September, 1894, Messrs. Lee and Moffett repur-
chased the property which gave them such an
excellent location and ample building space outside the city gate, and which, as mentioned above,
they had returned to the original owners a year
before.   After a stay of one month in the
pestilential city, the party returned to Seoul, and
it was on the Japanese transport steamer going
back that the noble-hearted Dr. Hall developed
typhus fever, from the effects of which he passed
to his reward a few days after his arrival in the
capital.

Messrs. Lee and Moffett returned in January,
1895.   This marked the permanent settlement of
the station in Pyeng-yang, although it was not
until May of the following year that, suitable
quarters having been prepared, they were joined
by Mr. Lee's family, when women's work received
an impetus through the coming of Mrs. Lee, and
meetings for women were begun.   Mr. Moffett
and Mr. Lee now settled down to their regular
work, which consisted of daily informal conver-

sation with inquirers, instruction of Christians, the holding of regular services, wide circulation of Christian literature and frequent journeys to the surrounding country in following up the work of native Christians and gathering in the fruits from their seed-sowing. From that time until the present the spread of the spirit of inquiry through the city and in ever-widening circles throughout the surrounding country has been something remarkable; and one of the most interesting features has been that each new convert has been seized with the spirit of the movement, and from the time of his conversion has become an active agent in the spread of the truth among his neighbors and friends. And so the work has grown until the mission workers in the station find their strength taxed to the utmost for the proper guidance of the movement and the suitable instruction of the inquirers. To be sure, the station has grown somewhat; but the reinforcements are mostly new missionaries, handicapped by their lack of knowledge of the language. Since the summer of 1895 they have had for a colleague J. Hunter Wells, M.D., who, in his commodious hospital, by his medical skill, has added material strength to the work. Last year they were joined by Rev. N. C. Whitmore, and the bride of Dr. Wells; and this year by Rev. W. B. Hunt and Miss Margaret Best, and the pressure of the work was felt to be so great that this fall Rev. and Mrs. W. M. Baird were detached from other work and

sent to Pyeng-yang.   All this looks to the opening of new stations in closer contact with the out-
lying work.   Nor have our brethren of the
northern Methodist Mission been idle; for their
mission station in Pyeng-yang has been reopened,
with Dr. and Mrs. E. D. Follwell and Rev. and
Mrs. W. A. Noble in charge.

In was in December, 1895, that Messrs. Lee and
Moffett were holding their winter class of a month
for the training of their leaders from the country
villages, and of the helpers of the missionaries,
and were taking them through a couple of the
books of the New Testament, seeking at the
same time to ground them in the faith and to
stimulate their zeal for Christian work.   Mrs.
Isabella Bird Bishop, the distinguished traveler
and authoress, happened at that time to visit
Pyeng-yang, and what she saw of the winter
class and of the Christian work in general in the
city made a deep impression upon her.   She has
thus expressed herself with her gifted pen:

"I am bound to say that the needs of Korea, or
rather the *openings* in Korea, have come to occupy
a very outstanding place in my thoughts.   *   *   *
The Pyeng-yang work which I saw last winter,
and which is still going on in much the same way,
is the most impressive mission work I have seen
in any part of the world.   It shows that the
Spirit of God still moves on the earth, and that
the old truths of sin, judgment to come, of the
divine justice and love, of the atonement, and of

the necessity for holiness, have the same power as in the apostolic days to transform the lives of men. What I saw and heard there has greatly strengthened my own faith.

"Now a door is opened wide in Korea, how wide only those can know who are on the spot. *Very many* are prepared to renounce devil-worship and to worship the true God if only they are taught how, and large numbers more who have heard and received the Gospel are earnestly craving to be instructed in its rules of holy living.   *   *   *

"I dread indescribably that unless *many men and women experienced in winning souls* are sent speedily, the door which the church declines to enter will close again, and that the last state of Korea will be worse that the first."

Since the visit of Mrs. Bishop to Pyeng-yang, in the winter of 1895, when what she saw impressed her so much, the work of the church in that city has had a still more remarkable development. The membership within that time has increased many fold, and the church building has had to be enlarged four times to meet the needs of the growing congregation, which is now so large that the preaching services for the men and women on the Sabbath have had to be held separately of late, simply because the edifice will not contain them all at one and the same time. Secretary Robert E. Speer and Mr. W. H. Grant, making a tour of our Presbyterian missions, in the summer of 1897 visited Pyeng-yang, and care-

fully studied the work. Mr. Speer has thus
expressed the impressions that were made upon
him: "After making all the necessary qualifications to cover the superficial, imitative and secular
Christians, and those who have come to Christ
without knowing what it means and who will drop
away when they learn; after making these reser-
vations, I am ready to say that I met in few
places in the world Christians so eager and intelligent, with such fresh spiritual experiences, with
such simple, practical faith, with minds so alert
and quickened by the Gospel. Our stay at
Pyeng-yang was very much like a week or fort-
night at a summer Bible school in America.
Every day, helpers unpaid by the mission came in
from the country to tell of fresh progress and
new congregations. There were no requests for
financial help. * * * The day we left Pyeng-
yang, thirty or forty of the native Christians
went with us through the rain many miles into
the country. We besought them to return home.
'No,' they said, 'you have come many thousands
of miles to see us; it is a small matter that we
should walk a few miles with you.' And so they
went with us until we came to a little thatched
church by the roadside, where, in the drizzling
rain they held a farewell meeting for us, thanking God for our visit, and commending us to His
love and care. It made us feel like Paul and his
company, when the elders of Ephesus came down
to take farewell of them at Miletus; and when a

turn of the road hid the little company from our
sight, we went on our way, thanking God, and I
frankly say with new faith and courage. It did
me more good than all the books on apologetics I
had ever read.''

To understand the growth and present status of
the work in the north of Korea, a few statistics
may be in order. In the spring of 1894, in
Pyeng-yang and its vicinity there were 10 baptized members of the church, with perhaps 40
catechumens. To the annual meeting of the
Presbyterian Mission in October, 1895, there
were reported an addition of 21 baptized members and 180 catechumens, with two church buildings, one wholly and one partially provided by
the Korean Christians, also two more churches
under way. In October, 1896, for the same
region there were reported to the mission an addition of 136 baptized members and 480 catechumens.

Including the work in the extreme north,
centering in Eui-Ju, the enrollment of the whole
station in the same year, 1896, was 207 members
and 503 catechumens, with 22 preaching-places
and contributions from the native congregations
amounting to 325 yen. Seven more church buildings were provided wholly or with slight help by
the Korean Christians. In September, 1897,
reports from the station showed further advance
as follows: There were 377 members and 1,723
catechumens, also 69 preaching-places, and a

partial report of money contributed amounting to 517 yen.   Also 14 new church buildings had been provided, through the efforts of the Korean Christians.   One word of Scripture explains this whole movement:

"THE GOSPEL IS THE POWER OF GOD UNTO SALVATION."

APPENDIX A.—MISSION STATISTICS FOR KOREA, 1896.

Name of Mission.	Date Begun.	Stations.	No. of Missionaries.	Helpers and Bible Women.	Out Stations where no Missionaries Reside.	Communicants.	Members Received (1 year).	Catechumens or Probationers.	No. of Organized Churches.	No. of Sabbath Schools.	No. of Pupils in Sabbath Schools.	Day Schools.	Pupils in Day Schools.	Boarding Schools for Boys.	Boarding Schools for Girls.	Pupils in Boys' Boarding Schools.	Pupils in Girls' B'd'g Schools.	Hospitals.	No. of In-patients Treated.	Dispensaries.	No. of Patients Treated.	Native Contributions. (Partial Report.) Yen.	Position.
American Presbyterian Mission (North)	1884	4	29	17	25	510	210	635	13	10	783	7	139	1	1	50	35	3	339	7	20,295	$796.44	Seoul, Gensan, Fusan, Pyeng-yang, (Taigu-prosp'tive).
American Presbyterian Mission (South).	1892	3	12	3	…	…	…	…	…	…	…	…	…	…	…	…	…	4	…	1	2,000	…	Seoul, Kunsan, Chunju.
Australian Presbyterian Mission	1889	1	5	2	…	…	…	…	…	…	…	…	…	…	1	…	9	…	…	…	…	…	Fusan.
Y. M. C. A. Mission of Canada	1890	1	2	…	…	…	…	…	…	…	…	…	…	…	…	…	…	…	…	…	…	…	
Korean Itinerant Mission	1889	1	1	…	…	…	…	…	…	…	…	…	…	…	…	…	…	…	…	…	…	…	Gensan.
American Methodist Mission (North)	1885	4	30	15	4	266	57	588	7	7	512	…	121	1	1	110	50	2	118	4	7,778	$647.37	Seoul, Chemulpo, Gensan, Pyeng-yang.
American Methodist Mission (South).	1896	1	2	…	…	…	…	…	…	…	…	…	…	…	…	…	…	…	…	…	…	…	Seoul, (Songdo prospective).
Ella Thing Memorial Mission (Baptist).	1895	1	4	…	…	1	…	3	…	…	…	…	…	…	…	…	…	…	…	…	…	.60	Seoul, (Kong-ju prospective).
Society for the Propagation of the Gospel.	1890	3	16	…	…	…	…	…	…	…	…	…	…	…	…	…	…	…	…	…	…	…	Seoul, Chemulpo.
Société des Missions Étrangères.	1784											21	204	2		271		3					Seoul, Chemulpo, Kang-wha.
		19	34	16	466	28,802	1250	…	18	…	…	21	204	2		271		3	118	4	7,778	…	

230

APPENDIX B.

Meeting Places	101
Communicants	932
Catechumens	2344
Added by Confession (11 months)	347
Sabbath Schools	18
Sabbath-school Scholars	1139
Church Buildings	38
Separate School Buildings	7
Students in Special Bible Training	101
Boys in Boarding Schools	35
Girls in Boarding Schools	38
Day Schools	15
Boys in Day Schools	141
Girls in Day Schools	25
Christian Pupils in Schools	33
United During Eleven Months	16
Total Native Contributions (partial report)	$971.12 (yen)

The Missionary Catalogue

OF

Fleming H. Revell Company

MISCELLANEOUS.

Robert Whitaker McAll,

Founder of the McAll Mission in Paris. A Fragment by
Himself, a Souvenir by his Wife. With Portraits and
other Illustrations. 8vo, cloth, $1.50.

"A volume of surpassing interest, as it must needs be, for it
tells the story of the most successful Christian effort that has ever
yet been put forward in the city of Paris . . . Few can understand, except imperfectly, the great service which Dr. McAll has
rendered to the work of evangelization in France."—*Christian
Work.*

Among the French Folk.

Sketches from Life. By E. H. MOGGRIDGE. 12mo, cloth,
60c.

Christian Life in Germany.

By Rev. E. F. WILLIAMS, D.D. 12mo, cloth, gilt top,
$1.50.

"It is a careful and scientific presentation of facts, based upon
thoughtful observation upon the field. It gives us a general sur-
vey; then the intellectual training; the moral and religious life;
the social and industrial movements; several chapters on missionary work, etc. Each chapter is carefully developed, and when one
lays down the book he feels he really knows the religious and social
condition of the great empire."—*The Standard.*

The Log of a Sky-Pilot;

Or, Work and Adventure on the Goodwin Sands. By
Rev. THOMAS S. TREANOR, M.A. Illustrated. 8vo, cloth,
$1.50.

'Mr. Treanor tells modestly, yet vividly, many of his experiences, some of which are very exciting."—*The Congregationalist.*

Heroes of the Goodwin Sands.

By Rev. THOMAS S. TREANOR, M.A. With many Illustrations. 8vo, cloth, $1.50.

"If boys who are searching for thrilling stories would read
books of this kind, they would be both profited and delighted."—
The Christian Intelligencer.

In the Path of Light Around the World.

A Missionary Tour. By Rev. THOMAS H. STACY. Pro-
fusely illustrated. Small 4to, cloth, $2.00.

Gospel Ethnology.

By S. R. PATTISON, F.G.S. Illustrated. *New edition.*
12mo, cloth, $1.00.

An ethnological study of the races to which the Gospel is being
carried.

Deinon Possession and Allied Themes.

Being an Inductive Study of Phenomena of Our Own Times. By Rev. JOHN L. NEVIUS, D.D., for 40 years a Missionary to the Chinese. With Bibliographical, Biblical, Pathological, and General Indexes. *Second edition,* with supplement. 8vo, cloth, $1.50.

"An interesting addition to psychological literature."—*The N. Y. Medical Journal.*

"He discusses the subject from the scientific as well as the religious side, has much to say about Spiritualism, and has made a significant and impressive volume. In our judgment, all candid readers will feel bound to admit that his position is probably correct."—*The Congregationalist.*

The Non-Christian Religions

Of the World. Living Papers Series. 12mo, cloth, $1.00.

Comprising six papers, by Sir W. MUIR, Prof. LEGGE, J. MURRAY MITCHELL, M.A., and Rev. H. B. REYNOLDS, D.D.

The Non-Christian Philosophies

Of the World. Living Papers Series. 12mo, cloth, $1.40.

Comprising eight papers, by Professors W. G. BLAKIE, NOAH PORTER, JAMES IVERACH, and J. RADFORD THOMPSON, and Rev. W. F. WILKINSON, M.A.

Mahomet and Islam.

A Sketch of the Prophet's Life from Original Sources, and a Brief Outline of his Religion. By Sir W. MUIR. With 8 Illustrations and a Map. *Third edition.* 12mo, cloth, $1.00.

"Sir William Muir has made a special study of Arabia before and during the life of Mahomet and is the first to rely almost exclusively for facts on the Arabic originals."—*The New York Times.*

The Caliphate.

Its Rise, Decline, and Fall. From Original Sources. By Sir W. MUIR, K.C.S.I., etc. With Maps. *Second edition,* revised. 8vo, cloth, $4.20.

The Beacon of Truth.

Testimony of the Coran to the Truth of the Christian Religion. Translated from the Arabic by Sir W. MUIR, Ph.D., etc. 12mo, cloth, $1.00.

Sweet First Fruits.

A Tale of the Nineteenth Century, on the Truth and Virtue of the Christian Religion. Translated from the Arabic, by Sir W. MUIR, Ph.D., etc. 12mo, cloth, $1.00.

The Growth of the Kingdom of God.

By Rev. SIDNEY L. GULICK. Illustrated with 26 diagrams.
12mo, cloth, $1.50.

Considers the relation of religion to civilization and to the
higher development of the human race. Some of the chapter head-
ings are: Preliminary Considerations and Conditions; The Numer-
ical Growth of Christian Adherents and of the Christian Nations;
Statistical Evidences of the Growth of the Kingdom of God in the
United States, and in England and Wales; Growth in Compre-
hension; Growth in Practice, etc.

The Early Spread of Religious Ideas,

Especially in the Far East. By Rev. JOSEPH EDKINS, D.D.
By Paths of Bible Knowledge Series. 12mo, cloth, $1.20.

The Rise and Spread of Christianity in Europe.

By W. H. SUMMERS. Present Day Primers. 16mo, flexible cloth, net, 40c.

Traces, in a clear and comprehensive way, the conquest of
Europe by Christianity.

Christ and the Heroes of Heathendom.

By Rev. JAMES WELLS, M.A. Illustrated. 12mo, cloth, 60c.

Æschylus, Socrates, Plato, Epictetus, Christ.

Nadya.

A Tale of the Steppes. By OLIVER M. NORRIS. Illustrated.
12mo, cloth, $1.25.

"The description of the life of the Stundists would alone repay
a perusal of the book."—*The Bookman.*

H. M. Stanley,

The African Explorer. By ARTHUR MONTEFIORE, F.R.G.S.
Illustrated. 12mo, cloth, 75c.

General Gordon,

The Christian Soldier and Hero. By G. BARNETT SMITH.
Illustrated. 12mo, cloth, 75c.

Sir John Franklin

And the Romance of the Northwest Passage. By G.
BARNETT SMITH. Illustrated. 12mo, cloth, 75c.

Fridtjof Nansen.

His Life and Explorations. By J. ARTHUR BAIN. Illustrated. 12mo, cloth, 75c.

Christian Missions and Social Progress

A Sociological Study of Foreign Missions

BY

Rev. I. S. Dennis, D.D.

Author of

"Foreign Missions after a Century"

With 50 full-page reproductions of original photographs

Two Vols., large 8vo, cloth, each $2.50

A new and notable book on foreign missions. Their influence is studied from the view-point of the sociologist, and results of fresh interest are brought forward. The evangelistic aim is duly honored as paramount; but special attention is devoted to the social significance of mission work as introducing stimulating and corrective ideals, giving promise of beneficent and far-reaching changes in the status of non-Christian peoples. The author has taken great pains to inform himself as to the social conditions of heathenism; and the thorough character of his investigations is apparent in the elaborate and admirably arranged chapter on the "Social Evils of the non-Christian World." The environment of Oriental civilizations, as well as the manners and customs of savage races, are studied. A searching review of the influence of the great ethnic religions of the world upon the higher life of society is given. An impressive exhibition of the adaptation of Christianity to purify the moral life of mankind and introduce regenerating forces into social evolution is presented. The service rendered by missions in the spheres of education, literature, philanthropy, social reform, and national development, are commented upon with insight and breadth of view. Their ministry as a stimulus to culture and a teacher of new and transforming social aspirations is dwelt upon with deep enthusiasm. The literary style is attractive and the illustrations beautiful.

"Dr. Dennis' new book, 'Christian Missions and Social Progress,' of which we have seen advance sheets, promises to be an invaluable encyclopedia of up-to-date information. No pains or expense have been spared to make it as complete and perfect as possible. It will have excellent maps, and an abundance of illustrations. Those who have read 'Foreign Missions After a Century,' will not be slow to become possessors of this still more valuable and interesting work as soon as it appears."—*The Missionary Review of the World.*

Missionary Biography Series.

"These are not pans of milk, but little pitchers of cream. If there are any better brief biographical sketches for general use as educators of the young, and as a means of general stimulation to the missionary spirit, we have not met them anywhere."—Rev. A. T. Pierson, D.D.

Illustrated, 12mo, cloth, each 75c.

Griffith John, Founder of the Hankow Mission, Central China. By Wm. Robson.

Robert Moffatt, the Missionary Hero of Kuruman. By David J. Deane.

James Chalmers, Missionary and Explorer of Rarotonga, and New Guinea. By Wm. Robson.

William Carey, the Shoemaker who became a Missionary. By Rev. John B. Myers.

David Livingstone. His Labors and His Legacy. By Arthur Montefiore, F.R.G.S.

Bishop Patteson, the Martyr of Melanesia. By Jesse Page.

Samuel Crowther, the Slave Boy who became Bishop of the Niger. By Jesse Page.

Thomas J. Comber, Missionary Pioneer to the Congo. By Rev. John B. Myers.

Lady Missionaries in Foreign Lands. By Mrs. E. R. Pitman.

John Williams, the Martyr Missionary of Polynesia. By Rev. James J. Ellis.

James Calvert; or, From Dark to Dawn, in Fiji. By R. Vernon.

Henry Martyn: His Life and Labors ; Cambridge—India—Persia. By Jesse Page.

David Brainerd, the Apostle to the North American Indians. By Jesse Page.

Madagascar, Its Missionaries and Martyrs. By W. J. Townsend, D.D.

Thomas Birch Freeman. Missionary Pioneer to Ashanti, Dahomey, and Egba. By Rev. John Milum.

Amid Greenland Snows; or, The Early History of Arctic Missions. By Jesse Page.

Reginald Heber, Bishop of Calcutta. By Arthur Montefiore.

Among the Maoris; or, Daybreak in New Zealand. By Jesse Page.

The Congo for Christ. The Story of the Congo Mission. By Rev. John B. Myers.

Missionary Heroines in Eastern Lands. By Mrs. E. R. Pitman.

Japan. Its People and Missions. By Jesse Page.

Missionary Annals.

This is an admirable series of outline sketches, remarkably complete for the size and more remarkably cheap. The volumes average 100 pages each, and are well printed and bound. They are intended especially for circulation in Missionary Circles, Societies, etc.

12mo, paper, each, net, 15c.; flexible cloth, each, net 30c.

1. **Memoir of Robert Moffat.** By M. L. Wilder.
2. **Life of Adoniram Judson.** By Julia H. Johnston.
3. **Woman and the Gospel in Persia.** By Rev. Thomas Laurie, D.D.
4. **Life of Rev. Justin Perkins, D.D.** By Rev. Henry Martyn Perkins.
5. **David Livingstone.** By Mrs. J. H. Worcester, Jr.
6. **Henry Martyn and Samuel J. Mills.** By Mrs. S. J. Rhea, and Elizabeth G. Stryker.
7. **William Carey.** By Mary E. Farwell.
8. **Madagascar.** By Belle McPherson Campbell.
9. **Alexander Duff.** By Elizabeth B. Vermilye.

Outline Missionary Series.

18mo, paper, each, 20c.

Madagascar. By Rev. J. Sibree, F.R.G.S.

Indian Zenana Missions. By Mrs. E. R. Pitman.

China. By Rev. J. T. Gracey, D.D.

Polynesia. By Rev. S. J. Whitmee.

South Africa. By Rev. J. Sibree, F.R.G.S.

Female Missionaries in Eastern Lands. By Mrs. E. R. Pitman.

India. In two parts. By Rev. E. Storrow.

The West Indies. By Mrs. E. R. Pitman.

Medical Missions. By Rev. John Lowe.

Revell's Missionary Library.

4 Volumes,

boxed,

8vo,

decorated cloth,

$5.00.

New, uniform edition, at greatly reduced prices, of the following standard Missionary works:

Persian Life and Customs. With Incidents of Residence and Travel in the Land of the Lion and the Sun. By Rev. S. G. Wilson, M.A., for 15 years a Missionary in Persia. With a Map and other Illustrations, and an Index. *Second edition.*

"Tells about the country and the people in a straightforward and intelligent fashion."—*The Brooklyn Eagle.*

From Far Formosa. The Island, its People and Missions. By Rev. G. L. MacKay, D.D., for 23 years a Missionary on the island. Edited by Rev. J. A. MacDonald. With 4 Maps, 16 Illustrations, and an Index. *5th thousand.*

"Undoubtedly, the man who knows most about Formosa.—*The Review of Reviews.*

Chinese Characteristics. With 16 full-page Illustrations and Index. By Rev. A. H. Smith, D.D., for 22 years a Missionary in China. *6th thousand.*

"The best book on the Chinese people."—*The Examiner.*
"A completely trustworthy study."—*The Advance.*

The Gist of Japan. The Islands, their People and Missions. By Rev. R. B. PEERY, A.M., Ph.D., of the Lutheran Mission, Saga. Illustrated.

Interesting, reliable and instructive.

RECENT PUBLICATIONS.

A Life for Africa. A Biography of the Rev. Adolphus C. Good, Ph.D., American Missionary in Equatorial West Africa. By Ellen C. Parsons, M.A., editor of "Woman's Work for Women." Illustrated. 12mo, cloth, $1.25.

"Like many other missionaries, he accomplished much of value in one or two departments of science, and an appendix to the work contains an account of his scientific labors by W. J. Holland, and a paper on the superstitions of the equatorial Africans, from his own pen. Such a book, wherever it goes, is a stimulus to missionary zeal, and is a work of real interest in itself."—*The Congregationalist.*

The Preparation for Christianity in the Ancient World. By R. M. Wenley, Sc.D. (Edin.), etc., Professor in the University of Michigan. 12mo, cloth, 75 cents.

"Man's unaided efforts to raise himself into communion with God, and their failure, leading at length to unparalleled moral obliquity and spiritual insolvency, cannot but afford fresh insight into the predestined deficiency of similar attempts at any time."—*From the Preface.*

Apostolic and Modern Missions. By Rev. Chalmers Martin, A.M. 12mo, cloth, $1.00.

The author, formerly a missionary to Siam, was invited to deliver the 1895 course of Students' Lectures on Missions before the students of Princeton Theological Seminary, in which institution he is an instructor. Repeated requests from the Faculty and students have resulted in the publication of the lectures in this permanent form.

Christianity and the Progress of Man. A Study of Contemporary Evolution in connection with the work of Modern Missions. By Prof. W. Douglas Mackenzie. 12mo, cloth, gilt top, $1.25.

"The book shows evidence of a thorough acquaintance with the literature of missions, and with the history of the progress of Christianity. It is another valuable addition to the missionary library, and is worthy of careful study."—*The Church at Home and Abroad.*

Missionary Methods for Missionary Committees. A Manual for Y. P. S. C. E., B. Y. P. U., and other young people's societies. With diagrams and charts by David Park. 16mo, cloth, net, 25 cents.

FLEMING H. REVELL COMPANY

CHICAGO: 63 Washington St.
NEW YORK: 158 Fifth Ave.
TORONTO: 154 Yonge St.

www.ingramcontent.com/pod-product-compliance
Lightning Source LLC
Chambersburg PA
CBHW031428020726
47499CB00005B/1643